C000089669

Starting Again
in
Silver Sands Bay
by
Karen Louise Hollis

First published in Great Britain in 2023

Copyright © Karen Louise Hollis

The moral right of Karen Louise Hollis to be identified as the author of this work has been asserted in accordance with the Copyright, Designs and Patents Act of 1988.

This book is a work of fiction. Names, characters, places and incidents are either a product of the author's imagination or are used fictitiously. Any resemblance to actual people living or dead, events or locales is entirely coincidental.

All rights reserved. No part of this publication may be reproduced, stored in a retrieval system, or transmitted in any form or by any means, electronic, mechanical, photocopying, recording, or otherwise, without the prior permission of both the copyright owner and the above publisher of this book.

To

Jessica Redland

A wonderful writer

And

An inspiring teacher

Starting Again in Silver Sands Bay

PROLOGUE

Five Years Earlier

Dan

Dan had just finished a completely normal day at work and was expecting a normal evening too. He'd been to four different places fixing various electrical items, the last house being owned by a lovely lady of eighty-two who had insisted he sit down for a cup of tea and biscuits before he left. So, as he got home and opened the door of their semi-detached, he was in a pretty good mood. Sadly, that wasn't going to last.

He noticed suitcases, bags and boxes piled up and then realised there was more noise than he was expecting. Instead of his wife Melanie chatting to their six-year-old son Freddie about his day, there were several men's voices. Soon he saw one, carrying some bags outside and packing them into a white van that was parked round the side of their house.

"Mel?" he called. He walked through the rooms, until he found her in the dining room at the back, directing two more men which furniture was going and which was staying. "Mel! What the fuck is going on?"

His wife looked at him open-mouthed. He rarely swore. "I'm leaving you, sugar!" She smiled that bright red lipstick smile he knew so well. "Don't worry, I'm not taking most of the furniture, just a couple of bits that are family heirlooms. I'm moving to California, so it's quite expensive to ship furniture over there. Not that money is going to be an issue for me from now on!"

Dan grabbed both her hands in an effort to keep her still. "Melanie! What on earth is going on? Who are you going to California with? I don't understand. What about Freddie?"

She shrugged, still failing to meet his eyes. "He'll stay here with you. He likes school, he's settled. Besides Edgar does a lot of travelling all over the world, so he's not going to want a young boy running round under his feet."

Dan felt like he was watching a film where the sound and vision wasn't quite in sync. "Edgar?"

"Yes," she said slowly. "I'm leaving you to be with Edgar." She was finally looking him straight in the eyes, as if she just had these thirty seconds to give him her full attention. Then she was off on her whirlwind again, running round, shouting instructions at the removal men.

"Where's Freddie?"

"At Sam's," she shouted back from somewhere.

He picked up his car keys and walked out the door. He drove over to Sam's and made small talk with his mum while Freddie got organised. He wasn't sure what they'd said, he was definitely on automatic. They stopped off for tea at Pizza Hut – Freddie's favourite and a rare treat, as Melanie thought pizza made her fat. His son was full of excitement, chatting happily about Sam's new toys they'd played with and thrilled to be having unexpected pizza.

When they got home, it was already seven o'clock and not far off his son's bedtime. It hit him that he'd be doing every bedtime from now on. Every bedtime, bath time, Parents' Evenings, school plays, sports days… But before they started the bedtime routine, he needed to have a talk with Freddie.

His son had been running round downstairs, checking in all the rooms and came back to his dad looking confused. "Where's Mum?"

Becki

Her husband Rob had only been given three months to live and he had already managed four, but they knew he was in his last hours now. By the time he'd started to feel any symptoms, hospital tests showed the cancer had already spread and there wasn't much the doctors could do.

All the family had come over. It took some of the strain off Becki, who had spent the last few months juggling work, caring for her husband and looking after their six-year-old daughter Jemima. Lizzie, Becki's younger sister, had been staying with them the last couple of weeks and she'd been an absolute godsend, both a great physical and mental support. She'd breezed in as usual and taken control of childminding duties, dog walking and housework, giving Becki precious time to spend with Rob and equally important time to do the things she'd forgotten about – eating, sleeping, taking care of herself.

The nurse had upped Rob's morphine and he was just sleeping now, his laboured breathing signalling he was still there, albeit a whisper of the big, strong, healthy man he'd once been. He was only forty-six, far too young, but Becki knew there was nothing fair about cancer. If anything about life was fair, Rob would have lived to a hundred, but it wasn't to be. He hadn't smoked, didn't drink to excess, he wasn't overweight. The doctors said it was bad luck, one of those inexplicable things that torture our lives and take away those we love prematurely.

Becki was empty of tears. In fact, she felt drained of everything, dried up inside and shrivelled away. She existed purely as a wife and a mother. Work had given her time off for compassionate leave, so she hadn't even been a teacher for nearly a month. What would be left of her when Rob died? How would she go on? But she knew she would live for Jemima; she would be her mother – and as much of a father as she could be too.

She was just making more cups of tea for the relatives when Lizzie came through. "I'll do those, Becki. I think you need to be with Rob now."

She understood the tone in her sister's voice, the unsaid words, and rushed through to the dining room that had become her husband's bedroom and bathroom. His mother was holding his hand, sobbing quietly and Becki went to his other side to hold his spare hand. Someone in the room was praying. It was probably his aunt; Becki couldn't think who else was religious. But then, people turned to God sometimes, in the worst of times – and this was definitely the worst.

She bent over to kiss Rob's lips, telling him she loved him, as she had every day they had been together, all those years of happiness that were being suddenly ended. So unfair. It made her angry. The nurse reached in to listen to his breathing and take his pulse, Becki wasn't quite sure what was happening now. She felt like she wasn't there, that everything was blurred, soft round the edges, like sleep-walking.

"He's not got long left," said the nurse. Becki couldn't remember her name. "I'm sorry." She could only nod in response, she had no words available.

There were three hard breaths to follow. Rob was struggling, it was obvious. His chest was shaking from the effort. His eyes remained closed and he didn't say a word. He was breathing and then he wasn't. They waited in silence, waiting for the next breath. But it didn't come.

The nurse reached over. "I'm sorry, he's gone."

There was no wailing, the room was strangely silent. Becki wondered if when her husband had stopped breathing, everyone else there had all ceased breathing too. In sympathy. The relatives filed past, some saying a quiet goodbye to Rob, touching his arm, his hand, stroking his hair. His mother kissed his cheeks and moved out of the room.

Soon only Becki was left by his bed. She had nothing more to say. She had nothing left inside her of any kind. She left the room in a haze of sorrow, and nodded at the nurse who came in and put a sheet over Rob's face with a respectful solemnity.

Becki walked back into the kitchen on autopilot. Lizzie reached over to give her a hug, tears on her cheeks, and caught her big sister as she fell.

CHAPTER ONE

July – Present Day

Becki

It was the fifth anniversary of losing him. Five long years. Sometimes it seemed like forever since they had last been together – the three of them – Rob, Becki and Jemima. The Gibsons. The Dream Team. The epitome of perfect family life. I mean, everyone said their marriage had been perfect when a partner died. It was often due to those rose-tinted glasses, but her marriage had been idyllic. Of course, they argued occasionally, but not over anything major, and they always made up before bedtime.

Oo other days, it all seemed unreal. She often woke up, still expecting him to be there beside her, his head on the pillow, his arm thrown across her in sleep. But he never was. He had left her, and she felt the empty side of the bed as deeply as a sharp cut every time.

If she'd been able to stop her life back then, just pause it at that point and never press play again, she would have done. But she couldn't be selfish, she had their daughter to look after. Jemima was eleven now and getting ready to go to secondary school in September. She owed it to her to stop looking back, and to start facing the future. "Moving on", they called it.

She had decided to take full advantage of the long school summer holidays this year. Being a teacher, she knew she was lucky to have the whole summer off and instead of moping around at home, everything reminding her of what she had lost, she was taking Jemima away – and Trudi, their ruby Cavalier King Charles Spaniel.

Jack Butler, the Deputy Head at Becki's school, owned a static caravan at Silver Sands Bay on the East Lincolnshire coast. Usually, he would be going there for the summer, but this time, his elderly mother was having an operation and he was staying in Yorkshire to look after her. This meant the caravan wasn't being used all summer. He had moaned about this in the staffroom and Becki asked if it was available to rent. It was only a spur of the moment thing. She didn't know she was going to ask until the words came out of her mouth. He'd been delighted and had offered her a really cheap deal, so everyone was pleased. Well, except maybe Jemima. You couldn't really tell with her. She was already demonstrating the worst aspects of being a teenager, even though she wasn't yet. It was like she was in a long dress rehearsal, practicing for all that was bad about teenagers. Her moodiness and silence irritated her mum the most. But she hoped the six weeks in the caravan would bring the two of them closer together.

So, here they were, car packed, leaving their home in Harrogate behind and travelling the 120-odd miles to the Lincolnshire coast. Trudi was happily looking out the window, her beautifully wavy spaniel ears moving slightly in the breeze coming through the half-opened windows. Jemima was in the front passenger seat, dog on her lap, looking at her phone. She'd just taken her scrunchie out and was absent-mindedly redoing her short red ponytail.

"Doesn't that make you feel car sick, having your head down like that all the time?" her mum asked.

She was answered with a shrug and a grunt, which was probably her way of saying no. It certainly seemed to imply a negative tone.

"I used to feel sick all the time, when I had my head down," continued Becki. "We used to go away on holiday, and I'd be in the back of the car reading my *Bunty* comic, or *Jackie* when I got a bit

11

older and after a while, I'd get a headache, feel nauseous and have to look out the window instead. It was annoying, waiting till we got there before I could finish reading." She gave a little laugh at the happy memory, but no sound came from her daughter's mouth in reply, only her fingernails clicking over the keys of her phone.

She gave up on her daughter joining in with any kind of conversation and switched the radio on to BBC Radio 2. Jeremy Vine's show was on. She liked him. He had intelligent conversations. And wasn't constantly on his phone.

Dan

Dan Armstrong turned off the radio. "I do like Jeremy Vine, but he doesn't half get some bloody annoying people on his show!"

Freddie laughed. This was a familiar conversation the two of them had. He was happy and relaxed, as was his dad. They were enjoying the journey and were both looking forward to spending the whole summer together.

"So, when was the last time you went to Nan and Grandad's caravan? Have I ever been there?"

"No, we stopped going just after you were born. I don't think your mum was ever that keen anyway, then after you came along, she put her foot down."

"Why?"

"She likes her luxuries, your mum. She wanted posh hotels, not back to basics. A portaloo and a shower block were a bit beneath her really."

"Guess she's happy now then, in America with her big house, her foreign holidays and her wealthy man."

"Hey, don't sound bitter, Freddie mate. We do okay, don't we? Your mum's settled, we're happy. You're growing up now, my little sidekick." He nudged him playfully with his left elbow. "Soon be at big school!"

"Secondary school, dad. Not big school. That makes it sound like I've just left nursery!"

"Hey, don't throw your toys out the pram!"

They laughed together, the son's higher pitched than his father's.

"What do you fancy doing at Silver Sands Bay then, Fred?"

"God knows! What is there to do there? I mean, six weeks is a long time!"

Dan was a self-employed electrician and had worked long hours in the previous six months, just so he could take the whole of the summer off work. His boy was growing up fast and he wanted to spend a good amount of time with him now, before it was all girlfriends and football practice and going into town with his mates.

"Well, I don't suppose it's changed too much in the last eleven years. Last time I went, there were several amusement arcades, a chippy, café, boating lake…"

"What kind of boats?"

"Pedalos, I think. Not big ones."

"And the beach, of course."

"Yes. Shame you're too big to build sandcastles now."

"That's okay. I'll watch Netflix on my phone while you're playing in the sand. I know who's the big kid here."

There was definitely some truth in that statement, Dan thought. He was rather looking forward to paddling in the sea and blocking up streams.

"Anyway," he continued to answer his son's question. "We're not far from a whole load of different seaside towns – Mablethorpe, Chapel St. Leonards, Cleethorpes…"

"And Skegness!"

"Oh yes, we'll definitely go to Skeg. There's lots to do there. Are you still up to challenging your old dad to a round of crazy golf?"

"Oh yeah, I'm up for that! As long as we get fish and chips afterwards."

"It's a deal!"

Becki

It was almost three o'clock in the afternoon and they were just approaching Silver Sands Bay. Jemima had been having a nap but woke up with perfect timing as they were entering the road which led into the caravan park.

"We're here, Jem!"

"It's raining!" her daughter moaned. "Typical!"

"Only a summer shower! It won't hang around long, then we can go out exploring."

Trudi put her front paws up against the side window, her tongue hanging out and her wavy tail wagging from side to side.

"At least the dog's excited," muttered Becki.

As she took the right turn into Tall Trees Caravan Park, she slowed her car down. "Look out for the place you book in, Jem. Jack said there's some sort of office you register at when you get there. So, they know which caravans are being used. I guess it's in case there are any fires or break-ins or something…"

"Oh. Won-der-ful…"

"Not that there will be. But, you know, regulations, Health and Safety…"

She looked from side to side until she found something which wasn't yet another caravan. This was a shed-like hut to one side with a handwritten sign saying RECEPTION nailed onto it. She had to admit she had expected something more impressive, but Jack had warned her it was all a bit cheap and cheerful.

She drove round, parked outside the shed, and got out. There was an elderly man sitting inside it, watching horse racing on a small television set.

"Hi," she said. "We're renting Jack Butler's caravan for the summer. I was told to check in here first. Name of Becki Gibson."

He barely took his eyes off the TV screen to check something in an A4 folder. He ticked a piece of paper then handed her over the keys, all without uttering a word. She took them off him and waited a few seconds, in case he had any wisdom to impart but no, his attention was fully back to the racing.

"Thanks then," she said to the back of his head. "Lovely talking to you."

Dan

It was about five past three by the time they got there. "There it is! Tall Trees Caravan Park!" Freddie was pointing to the sign that his dad had already seen.

"Well spotted, son! Now we have to go and sign in, apparently. Some bloke in a hut. But first of all, your Nan suggested we go to the little supermarket to stock up on bits. Then we can get everything sorted out in the caravan and have a sandwich and a cuppa, without having to rush straight out for provisions."

"Clever Nan! Plus, it's raining, so it'd be good to just settle in for an hour or so, before we go off exploring!"

"Exactly my thoughts."

Dan pulled up in front of the supermarket, which was situated to one side of the caravan park. There were only three parking spaces, but they were all empty. Most of the customers must walk from the caravan site, rather than drive in from elsewhere.

"Nan says this is the nearest you get to a Tesco here, but it's a bit more expensive, not being a big chain, so don't go mad!"

They walked in. The shop was surprisingly well-stocked for its size. Dan grabbed one of the metal shopping baskets and headed for the first aisle, spotting his usual brand of tea bags. Freddie went towards the magazine section, its bright colours and enticing front covers attracting his attention.

They met up at the second aisle, Dan's basket already half full. Freddie was holding the latest editions of a gaming magazine and a football one. Grinning cutely at his dad, his smiling face at a jaunty angle, his dad nodded and said "Okay. Guess they'll keep you quiet. Especially if the phone signal's patchy."

"The phone signal's patchy?"

"Have I raised a parrot?" he laughed. "Yes, it's officially 'intermittent' on the site. Come on, we'll find other things to do. And there's a phone box not far away, if you're desperate to ring your mates or something."

"A phone box? Is it the 1970s in Silver Sands Bay?"

"Nothing wrong with phone boxes, son."

"So, the caravan site won't have Netflix then, will it?"

"No, it won't." He sighed. "Go on then, go and get yourself another magazine…"

Almost fifty quid lighter, but with a few days of food and drink essentials, Dan drove them round to the reception hut and checked them in. With keys in hand and following the site owner's curt directions, they drove slowly down towards the caravan that would be their home for the next six weeks.

Becki

They parked outside their designated caravan. Becki walked round it, admiring its sea-blue coloured paint and the pale blue curtains with a subtle shell design on them.

"Ah, this is nice. Very tasteful."

"Is '80s Sea Décor a thing then?"

Becki ignored her moody daughter, realising she was 'hangry' and needed feeding as soon as possible. Her dad had been the same, bless him, she'd always known when his blood sugar was getting low, and he needed sustenance.

"What's that smell?" Jemima sniffed the air loudly.

"Sea? Salt?"

"You make it sound like a bag of Walkers crisps, Mum! I think it's chips, is there a chippy nearby?"

"Yes, I'm pretty sure there is. Let's unpack the car, have a look round the caravan – "

"That won't take long. It's hardly a luxury hotel suite."

"– then we'll take a walk and find the chippy."

Trudi was just finishing a much-needed wee on the grass as Becki unlocked the door with the key the site owner had given her at Reception. There were two small steps going up then the door opened straight into a small kitchen, sink in front, cooker to the left, with a microwave, toaster and kettle on a small area to the right.

She walked into the room, Trudi getting under her feet as she bounded round her new space sniffing everything excitedly. The main area to the left of the kitchen was the big lounge. It had a TV, gas fire, pull-out dining table and two collapsible chairs, plus some shelves and storage cupboards. The three sides of the room had long sofas which could also be pulled out for extra beds if need be.

"Well, this looks rather nice, Jem. I can see us settling here, watching TV, reading, playing cards and board games…" She laughed at her daughter's glare. "That's how I spent my childhood. We didn't have the internet or mobile phones or Netflix."

Jemima rolled her eyes and walked through the kitchen to look at the rest of the caravan. There were two bedrooms – one double, one single – both small, but adequate. The beds looked comfy enough and had warm duvets and several fluffy pillows piled on top.

Becki was behind her, peering around her daughter to have a look. "Ooh I like how the pale blue sea theme is echoed here. Pretty bedding."

"The single room's small."

"Well, yes, because it's a single bed. You're in that one, the double's mine. I like to starfish. Plus, I'll have Trudi with me, and she takes up more room than you'd expect for a little spaniel."

Trudi had first spent the night in Becki's bed the day that Rob had died. It was just like the dog realised what had happened and that her warmth would be a comfort amongst all the grief. She had been there every night since, snuggling up to her mistress to provide what help she could.

Jemima had just opened the final door to what looked like a cupboard. "What on earth's this thing?"

Becki peered round her shoulder again. "Ah, that's the loo. It's a chemical toilet."

Jemima lifted up the lid and covered her nose, making over-the-top vomiting sounds.

"God, Jem, it's not that bad. It's just chemicals, it's clean! It's not been used for ages."

"I'm not using that."

"Fine. You know that big brick building we drove past, about a five-minute walk away?"

Her daughter nodded. "That's the toilet and shower block. If you fancy walking down there at four o'clock in the morning for a wee, feel free. Personally, I'm happy to have an indoor loo, regardless of what it looks like and how chemically it smells."

Jemima huffed off and plonked herself on a sofa. "And it smells musty in here!"

"We'll open the windows when we get back from our walk. Air it out a bit. I told you, no-one's been here for ages."

Becki went to the car to bring their suitcases in. "We can unpack properly later. I'll just bring these in here for now, then drive the car round the side, where the sign said to park your vehicles. There's some big car park thing there just for residents. Then we'll go and find that chip shop and try to fill that grumpy tummy of yours."

Jemima was twiddling with her phone, pushing buttons in between deep sighs.

"Mum!" she screeched, making Becki jump.

"What the f-? Er, flip? You nearly gave me a heart attack!"

"Mummmmm!" Jemima wailed. "There's no Wi-Fi!"

Dan

They parked outside the dark brown and white static caravan that was to be their home for the summer. Opening the boot to get out their cases, Dan said "I think we'll be okay here, what do you think? I mean, it's not the most modern accommodation, but it suits your Nan and Grandad, and we aren't too fussy, are we?"

"Yeah, looks fine. At least we'll stay dry. Not like when we went camping in Wales that time!" They laughed.

"Your mum insisted she could do the tent by herself, didn't she?"

"It was like having a shower! We had to check into that cheap hotel after one night."

"And your mum wasn't happy about that either, was she?"

"Well, it's just us two now, Dad. We don't have so many airs and graces. Let's see if we can holiday without complaining!"

"Ha! We'll see. Come on, Freddie, give me a hand with these bags."

Dan unlocked the front door, and they went up the two steps and straight into the kitchen. Dan went into the rooms on the right and put his suitcase in the double bedroom and his son's bags in the single bedroom. He took his anorak off and hung it over the bedroom door to dry.

"These bedrooms are a bit small, but we'll be in the lounge most of the time."

"Yep, I'm just trying out the sofas. Bit basic, but comfy enough. And the telly's not too small."

Dan was unpacking the supermarket shop into the kitchen space. "Have you checked out the loo though?"

Freddie came through and Dan indicated the door to the right of him, in-between the kitchen and the double bedroom. Freddie opened it, looked and laughed. "Well, that's better than going out to that old toilet block in the middle of the night."

"That's what I thought."

Dan put the kettle on, opening all the cupboards and drawers to find out where the cups, plates and cutlery were kept. Everything seemed to be organised logically. "Oh, I remember these mugs!" He showed Freddie a tinted glass see-through mug in a fetching shade of green.

"Wow! Very 1970s, Dad."

"Maybe even 1960s."

"Cool though."

"Very. Right, cup of tea in one of these then, son?"

"Absolutely! And what did you get for sandwiches?"

"Cheese or ham."

"Ah, great. Cheese please." He stretched his legs out along one side of the sofa, his bright red trainers contrasting with the pale floral pattern underneath him and pressed a few buttons on his phone. "Dad!"

"Um?"

"What's the Wi-Fi code?"

"Ah. I don't think there is one."

"No code?"

"No Wi-Fi."

"Wow! It really is the 1970s…"

Becki

The chip shop was easy to find, just off the caravan site and the second shop on the right, after a kind of corner shop they'd explore another time. Their priority right now was food. Becki's stomach was rumbling as she smelt the familiar tang of fish and chips quite a while before the actual shop came into view. She hadn't eaten since breakfast and that felt like a long time ago now.

Luckily the rain had stopped because the queue was out the door. Jemima pulled her hoody sleeves down past her wrists though, as if it was freezing. She continued to poke the buttons on her phone to try to find some internet or a mobile hotspot or something. Anything! Becki suspected the under-her-breath muttering she could hear included some choice swear words, but she decided not to bother having that discussion right now.

The shop was quite big. As well as the food counters and tills on the left, there was a seating area that housed about four tables with chairs around them and a high bench for customers to sit at. These were already full; it was obviously the place to come for your tea in Silver Sands Bay! Quite wittily, it was called The Inn Plaice, she noticed – and indeed it was, by the look of the trade they were doing, and it wasn't even five o'clock yet.

As the queue moved, they could see all the food on offer, metal trays filled with frying chips, shelves of sausages and a variety of battered delights. Becki decided to get fish, chips and mushy peas. "What do you want, Jem?"

"Are the chips vegetarian?" Jemima asked the woman behind the counter, who was looking a bit frazzled.

"Yes, they're cooked in vegetable oil, separate from the fish."

23

"Great. I'll have chips and mushy peas then. Do you do halloumi at all?"

"Erm, no, just what's written on the board." She indicated behind her where items were written up, including the fish of the day.

"How much is that?" interjected Becki, preventing her daughter from asking anything more and holding the queue up any further. They moved to one side while they waited for their order to be wrapped up. "Since when have you been vegetarian, Jem?"

"Since last Wednesday."

"You never mentioned it."

"You never asked."

Becki was beginning to think it was going to be a very long summer holiday. She should have brought more books.

Dan

"That dog's making a lot of noise for a little thing!"

Dan looked out the small kitchen window. "Where is it? I can certainly hear it! It sounds like a small dog."

"Yeah, a small dog with a big bark. It's over to the left, in the row of caravans in front of us. The blue one."

Dan came through to the lounge and looked to where his son was pointing. "Oh yes, I see it. A little spaniel. Poor thing. It's probably not used to being left by itself. Hopefully its owners will be back soon."

He went back to the kitchen and finished the drying up and putting away.

"Right, are you ready to go out and explore the place?"

They walked up past the uninviting looking toilet block, Freddie trying not to breathe as he went by. All they could see everywhere else they looked were rows and rows of caravans. The outsides were painted differently, but they all looked to be the same size and shape. Some had shiny new paint jobs and bright curtains, whereas others looked a bit neglected with faded paint colours and pale, washed-out looking curtains.

"Are these caravans all on the one site, Dad? There are loads of them, as far as you can see!"

"No, there are two sites merged here. This one, the one we're staying on, is older and then, the one you can see over there is a newer one."

They turned left and onto the main street in Silver Sands Bay. The seafront was right ahead of them, with arcades and shops on either side of the road.

"Well, we've eaten so we don't need the chippie. What do you fancy doing first?"

"Arcades?"

There were big amusement arcades on both sides of the road. The one on the right went all the way round the corner, its noisy machines and the dropping of coins echoing out into the street as they walked by. They crossed over and looked at the buildings on the left side. There was a pub advertising a quiz night, darts tournament and a drag queen. A couple of outdoor fairground rides jutting out onto the path, including a little one with blue and red ladybirds, toddlers sitting in them grinning, as the ride went round slowly to unrecognisable over-loud music.

They walked past these and into the arcade. Suddenly everything became much louder as pinball machines and slot machines competed to attract punters with their noise and lights. Further on, at the back, there was a café selling mainly burgers, but with quite a range of hot and cold drinks.

Opposite, there was an area set back a bit. This contained a couple of snooker tables, three pool tables and an air hockey table. There was a serious-looking snooker match taking place there, two men in their forties taking long considered pauses before trying their shots.

"I wonder if that's a local tournament or something. It all looks quite official."

"Yes, it could be. We'll save the snooker for another day then. Fancy a game of pool, Dad?"

"Absolutely! I'll just get some change. I doubt they'll take ten-pound notes."

"Ooh, aren't you flash with your ten-pound notes? In that case, if you're feeling rich, Dad, can I myself get a Coke?"

His dad handed him over some money. "Get us one too, please, son. If I'm not here, I'll meet you over at the pool table."

Becki

"I hope Trudi's been okay, Jem. Once we've eaten, we'll go and get her and take her out with us. We can walk round the rest of the area and up to the seafront."

She was holding the carrier bag and the smell was reminding her how hungry she was. Mind you, chips did that. She'd be comfortably full up, then someone walked past with chips, and she would be craving them. It was a magical smell, especially at the seaside.

As they got a couple of caravans away from theirs, they realised they could hear barking. "Oops!" muttered Becki, quickening her pace. "Sounds like someone's been missing us!" She opened the door and was greeted by a leaping, squealing bundle of fluff. "Blimey! You'd think we'd been out weeks!"

Trudi did a quick wee on the grass, then they all went inside. Becki gave the dog her tinned food then got the plates and cutlery out so her and Jemima could eat their meals. Jemima pulled out the little table and chairs and they sat down. It wasn't long before they were joined by Trudi at their feet, looking up eagerly with her tongue hanging out and her big brown eyes.

After their meal, they put the excited Cavalier King Charles Spaniel on her lead and took a walk past the shops and amusement arcades and up the ramp onto the seafront. It was still a bit cold out and it was quite breezy up there, without any shelter from the wind. Jemima put her hood up and Becki zipped up her coat. The sea was quite calm, but dark grey. No-one was swimming in it now, but there were lots of dog walkers and a few elderly couples taking a leisurely stroll.

"The families must have gone inside to eat their tea and get the little ones ready for bed," observed Becki. "We'll just walk along here for now; we can go on the beach another day. Preferably when it's a bit warmer."

Jemima nodded and they walked off together towards the left, where there were signposts pointing towards a boating lake. It was about a five- or ten-minute walk before they could see it all spread out below them.

"That'll be perfect on a day when it's sunny weather," Becki pointed. There was a big yellow bouncy castle, a big slide saying ASTROGLIDE on the top, a café or two, some kind of shops – she couldn't quite tell from this high up - plus the lake itself. She could see people still walking round it, at varying speeds. They were probably trying to get their daily steps in, she thought, guiltily looking at the space on her left wrist where she'd worn her Fitbit until the novelty had worn off.

Jemima made a non-committal kind of grunting noise and turned her attention back to the beach. "Why is it called Silver Sands Bay?"

"Because the sands are a pretty silver colour, not golden like in some parts of the country or pebbly."

"They don't look silver to me. They look kind of – well, grubby!"

"I can't see people flocking to a seaside town called Grubby Sands Bay though, can you? Whatever you do, love, don't apply for a job with the Lincolnshire Tourist Board."

They turned back and walked the way they'd come in silence, until they were outside the shop next to The Inn Plaice. "Do you want some money to get a magazine or something? That shop seems to be part newsagents."

"Nah, I think I'll watch TV tonight."

"You do know they won't have Netflix, don't you? It'll just be terrestrial TV, I should think."

"Oh, for Gods' sake!"

Jemima made a big sighing noise that sounded like it was heaved all the way up from her toes to her mouth before she released it. She put her hand out for the money being offered and dragged her feet into the shop, leaving Becki rolling her eyes at her back. Just then, Trudi decided to do a poo on the pavement. As Becki pulled out a poo bag, she hoped things were going to go better the next day. This holiday hadn't got off to the greatest of starts.

CHAPTER TWO

Dan

Still half-asleep and only wearing his Marvel Avengers pyjama shorts, Dan got up and put the kettle on. He needed coffee. The bed hadn't given him the best night's sleep, but his body clock was telling him he should get up and start the day. He opened the curtains in the lounge and was greeted with sunshine. He checked his phone. 8:13 a.m. Still no Wi-Fi. He wasn't expecting anyone to contact him though, so he wasn't too bothered. A man at the arcade the previous evening had told him Skegness was the best place for an internet signal, so he had promised Freddie they'd go there in the next day or two, just to check if anything important had happened while they'd been offline. It was scary really, how much they all relied on the internet these days.

The caravan site was pretty quiet at the moment. He could only hear a young child laughing in the distance and birdsong coming from the long-established trees that gave the caravan park its name. He stretched out on one side of the sofas and sipped his coffee, enjoying the thought of not having to do anything in particular. It was liberating. He wasn't clock-watching, running from job to job, fixing one old lady's lightbulb and planning to get home early, then getting an emergency call about the power going off in a rural pub that needed repairing right now.

He could work to his own schedule for the summer, not everyone else's and of course, no work was involved for those six weeks. Just play. Rest and relaxation and quality time with his only child. What more could he want? He didn't need some flash foreign holiday in temperatures of thirty-five degrees. Good old-fashioned caravan holidays on the British coast were much more his sort of thing.

He was also quite enjoying not having an internet connection. He didn't have to worry about the news, check Twitter or his Facebook feed, or see photos of his ex-wife sunning herself somewhere on Instagram. In fact, he should go back to that supermarket and buy himself a novel or two; it'd be good just to let himself sit and read. He hadn't finished a book for a long time, but he'd loved reading all his life. These days, there was always something more pressing to do – an invoice to email, tea to cook for him and Freddie, bills to pay, someone to say Happy Birthday to on Facebook.

Yes, he'd nip back to that supermarket when Freddie was up, find a good thriller to get stuck into. Placing his empty coffee cup on the floor beside him, he decided to shut his eyes for a few more minutes. Because he could.

Becki

It was already ten o'clock and Jemima was still fast asleep. Becki had drunk a cup of tea – the first one of the day was always the best – and let the dog out and now she was ready to start going out and doing something, but what was there to do inside the caravan? There wasn't any housework, they hadn't been here long enough to make a mess. There was no internet, and she couldn't go anywhere and leave her daughter by herself at only eleven years old. It wasn't like their Cavalier King Charles Spaniel would protect her from intruders either. A bit of fuss from anyone and the dog would be flat on her back, hoping her belly was tickled.

She decided to have a look in all the little cupboards and drawers in the lounge. Most were empty, but she found a few treasures including a game of Chinese Chequers and a pack of playing cards. Many an hour of her childhood had been spent playing both of these, so she kept them out on the side. She'd loved Patience or Sevens – decades before it had become a mobile phone game called Solitaire – and Round The Clock Patience. She'd played Drawing the Well Dry countless times with her dad, though she had no idea how to play it nowadays. Maybe she could interest Jemima in a game of something? It might take her mind off the lack of internet for a few minutes.

She went to her bedroom to get her book – the latest Heidi Swain novel – and was about to sit back on the sofa when she saw some people walking past. It was a tall, slim man with short, dark hair who looked to be around her age and what looked to be his son. They were chatting happily and laughing, and she realised she was smiling watching them. She wished her relationship with Jemima was as easy as their relationship seemed to be. Sometimes she felt she hardly knew her daughter at all.

The man turned slightly to look at something the boy was pointing out and Becki caught a better look at his face. "Ooh, he's not bad looking, not bad looking at all!"

"You eyeing up some random now, Mum?"

"Oh, hi love, I didn't hear you get up."

"No, you were too busy perving over some bloke!" She laughed, heading over to the kitchen area and putting the kettle on for her own cup of tea. Like her mother, she needed a cuppa to get going first thing in the morning.

"He had some boy with him, Jem, looked about your age. Maybe you can make a friend here?"

"Hmm. Maybe. There were just the two of them? No woman?"

"Well, yes. No woman with them."

"Maybe he's a single parent like you?"

"Who knows? His wife could be back at the caravan."

"We'll have to keep an eye out."

"You are funny, Jem. Are you trying to matchmake me or something?"

Jemima walked in with her cup of tea and sat down.

"You're fifty, Mum. Don't you ever think about finding another boyfriend sometime?"

"Not really. I still love your dad."

"So do I, and that's not ever going to change. But, well, you know..." She took an audible breath, and her words came out in a rush. "He's been dead five years; you can't put your life on hold forever."

"Jem!"

"No, listen. I won't be living with you for decades and decades and when I've left home, I don't want to think of you on your own, in your early sixties or whatever and just you and Trudi. You need to have your own life again."

Becki tried to think of something to say, but everything she thought of sounded wrong. She looked at Jemima sipping her tea and realised there was a lot going on in her daughter's head that she hadn't given her credit for.

"I'll go and get myself another cuppa, while the tea's hot," she said, heading into the kitchen. Rinsing her cup under the cold water tap, she put a tea bag in on automatic, pouring the still-hot water and getting the milk out of the fridge. She didn't know what to say, what to do. She needed some time to think, to process what her daughter had said. Was she right about moving on? And when had Jemima become so wise and grown up?

She took her tea back into the front room. "Shall we go out with the dog in about half an hour?"

"Okay, I'll just grab something to eat and get dressed."

Dan

They didn't have much of a choice of decent novels in the little supermarket. Most of the books were obviously romance types aimed at women, judging by their pastel colours and lovey-dovey illustrations, but there were some titles he was interested in. Ignoring all the macho war and action type books he couldn't stand, he found some thrillers and bought a T. M. Logan he'd hadn't read and one by an author he hadn't heard of, but the blurb reeled him in. It sounded like an interesting premise for a psychological thriller anyway.

Freddie still hadn't read all his magazines, so he just added a couple of bottles of lemonade and his favourite cereal to the shopping basket.

As they walked back through the caravan park, Freddie said "Oh look, it's that cute little dog again, the one that was barking!"

It was standing up on its back legs looking out the window at them, its tail wagging increasingly faster as they got nearer to it.

"It's doing that doggy smiling thing!"

"It certainly is!"

"We should get a dog, Dad. I'm about the only kid in my class that hasn't got a pet."

"I have thought about it, but I just don't get enough time to take it for walks and it'd be at home all day on its own. But, you know, maybe in the future. Never say never… Unless you fancy something a bit less high maintenance. Maybe a goldfish or a hamster?"

"It's not the same, Dad!"

As they turned the corner, Freddie noticed a movement in his peripheral vision. Looking at the caravan window again, he saw a girl in there this time, about his age with a short red ponytail. She gave him a sort of half wave and he raised his hand to her, smiling.

Dan turned to see who he was waving at. "Oh, she's with that dog, is she?"

"Must be."

"She looks about your age. You might have a friend to play with then, while you're here. Save you being with your old dad all the time."

"Dad!" he groaned. "We don't really *play* nowadays, that's for babies. We hang out."

"Ah, sorry, mate, a friend to *hang out* with then…"

They walked up the steps to their caravan and went inside. After a quick drink of lemonade, Dan said "So, sandwiches for dinner or chippy chips?"

"Chippy chips! No contest."

"Come on then."

Becki

As soon as they were ready, Becki, Jemima and Trudi set out back along the same street, this time passing the chip shop and heading past the amusement arcade that went round the corner. They followed it this time, seeing what was further up in that direction. The arcade ended and after that was a huge caravan site that backed onto theirs.

"Those caravans look a bit posh, don't they, Mum?"

They certainly did. They were bigger than the one they were staying in and as they walked past, they could see they had wider sofas with proper cushions, rather than the thin three-sided sofas in theirs. There was a big television fixed to the wall and it looked like they had a proper separate dining area too, instead of just the lounge.

"Mmm, very nice. Bet it's got three bedrooms too, by the length of it!"

"Shame that Deputy Head of yours didn't own one of these!"

"Yes, these do look more high-end…"

"I bet they don't have chemical loos either."

"They might even have their own showers in those!"

"Ooh! Fancy!"

They laughed and kept on walking. The caravans continued; the site was enormous. At the end, they found a small arcade with a bingo game going on. The sign on the door said DOGS WELCOME, so they went inside. An attractive dark-haired man of an indeterminate age was calling the numbers out into a microphone - all two little ducks, unlucky for some thirteen and Rishi's Den – Number Ten.

"I used to love prize bingo as a kid," whispered Becki. "Let's have a go. It might be fun."

They sat down and waited for the next round to start, getting their money ready and enjoying the easy banter of the charismatic bingo caller. Trudi sat down nicely at their feet, sniffing for any bits of food left on the floor.

Half an hour later, they left with a Troll that Jemima had chosen from the wins they'd accumulated and a big box of Maltesers to share. She had to agree with her mum that it had been lots of fun, even if the internet wasn't involved.

Reassuring the bingo caller they'd be back in the next few days, they continued with their walk for a bit, but there was nothing to see after that, it was like Silver Sands Bay finished at the bingo. They turned back, crossed the road and walked up onto the seafront again.

"Beach?" she asked Jemima.

"Why not?"

Trudi excitedly pulled on the lead, sniffing the fresh sea air through her little black nose.

"That's a yes from Trudi!"

This time, they ventured down on to the beach, their feet sinking slightly into the soft sand. It was early afternoon and despite being July, it wasn't really T-shirt weather, but they were warm enough in their thin anoraks. The sea was out, so they walked all the way up to it and let Trudi have a little paddle and a play in the shallow waves lapping back and forth on the pale sand. She barked at a particular wave, jumped on it, and then couldn't work out where it had gone.

"Silly dog! You squashed it, it's under your paws!"

They laughed at her, and she barked. "She's joining in now!"

As they walked up to a rock pool, they saw two young kids and presumably their mum sitting around it with buckets, spades and nets. It sounded like they had just found a crab, by the squealing coming from the young girl who didn't seem to know whether to be excited or terrified. "If you don't touch it, it won't bite you," reassured the woman, smiling at Trudi as she came to have a sniff, though keeping a wary distance. She wasn't sure what to make of the crab either.

After an hour or so, they decided to head back. As they walked past the café part of the arcade, Becki said "Ooh, I fancy a coffee. Do they let dogs in?" They peered in through the windows but couldn't see any dogs or any signs. "Shall I give you some money? If you can get me a coffee and whatever you want, and we'll just drink them out here."

Jemima went inside, walking past the flashing, bleeping machines and heading to the quieter café area. As she carried her Coke and the coffee back through the arcade, she saw a man and a lad playing pool. As she got nearer, she recognised them from earlier when they'd gone past the caravan. The boy obviously recognised her too, as he smiled and said "Hi!"

"Oh hello! Are you winning?"

"I am actually, beating Dad 2-1."

His dad had just narrowly missed potting a ball and sighed, grinning at Jemima, and offering his hand to shake. "Yeah, he's beating me again. I'm Dan, by the way. You've got that gorgeous little dog, haven't you?"

"Trudi. Yes, she's outside with Mum. We didn't know if dogs were allowed in."

"No, I haven't seen any here."

"That's what we thought."

"I'm Freddie," the boy introduced himself.

"Jemima. Jem. My mum's called Becki. With an 'i' at the end, not a 'y'. Anyway, I'd better get back or Mum will get a cold cup of coffee."

"Sure. She won't want that. Right, well, we'll see you around then, Jemima!"

"Sure will. Bye!"

"Bye, Jem!"

She walked through the rest of the arcade and presented her mum with the coffee. It had just started spitting with rain and she was looking a bit cold, leaning against the arcade wall for shelter.

"I thought you'd got lost!"

"No, I found our friends in there."

They started walking off slowly towards their caravan site, sipping their drinks, and letting Trudi have a good explore on the end of the lead.

"Do we have any friends here?"

"You know, random handsome guy and his son."

"Ah, those friends. Are they nice?"

"Yes, they seem lovely. The man's called Dan and the son's Freddie. They like our dog."

"Well, that's good then."

"It's a start!" Jemima grinned at her mum.

"Oh no, my daughter's stirring!" Becki started singing *Matchmaker* from *Fiddler on the Roof*, as they walked back to their summer home. "Matchmaker, matchmaker, make me a match…"

Dan

A couple of days later, it was lovely and sunny, so Dan and Freddie agreed to go to Skegness for the day. It was only a ten-minute drive. Dan parked in one of the car parks not far from the seafront and as he turned the car engine off, both their mobile phones began pinging with seemingly endless notifications. They immediately stared at their screens, trying to catch up with all the information being thrown at them.

"Max says the new Minecraft update is good," Freddie informed his dad. "Ruby's sent me some photos of her new puppy and I've had six missed calls from Mum. Shall I ring her back?"

"I've had a load from your mum too. I'm enjoying my holiday, my little bit of peace and quiet and I don't really want to be brought down by some stupid argument with your mother. Nor do I much fancy hearing her telling me how amazing her new life is."

"Fair enough."

"You can ring her if you want. I mean, she is your mum."

"Nah. I'm not ready to listen to more news about her and The Amazing Edgar on their world tour. Maybe later."

After having caught up with the BBC News headlines, football scores and their various social media accounts, they wandered off along the seafront. There were hotels the other side of the street, some looking rather plusher than others. You could tell the ones that were aimed at the elderly couples and those advertising cheap alcohol and live music, aimed at the younger partygoers. Dan had a bit of a shock realising these days he'd prefer the quieter, more subdued accommodation aimed at the over-sixties. And he wasn't quite fifty yet.

Dan remembered the crazy golf was at the end of the long road they were on, so they took a slow, steady stroll in that direction, looking around at everything the famous seaside resort had to offer on this late July day.

On the seafront side of the road, there were a variety of amusement arcades interspersed with ice cream kiosks, candy floss booths, stalls selling souvenir sticks of rock and coffee outlets. As they passed one selling doughnuts, their noses were both drawn in by the appealing sugary smell and as if enchanted, Dan ended up buying five doughnuts to share, a coffee for him and a lemonade for Freddie. They leant against the wall, chewing and swallowing, looking out across the busy beach and into the sparkling sea beyond.

"I always think that looks like a painting," commented Dan, as he finished his first sticky doughnut. He pointed in front of them, waving the brown paper bag containing the rest of the overly sweet treats. "There's like a straight line between the sea and the sky, like someone's just put a brushstroke there to remind them to finish off the painting properly later."

Freddie giggled. "Hey, you'll be an art expert next, on one of those BBC2 programmes." He put on a posh accent. "Oh yes, you can really see the meaning behind the textures and the colour scheme the painter has used here. This black swirl shows his emotional turmoil and this pawprint is where his cat walked across the canvas!"

Dan spluttered a bit of coffee onto the sand. "Ah, you're a born entertainer, you are, son. You ought to be on the stage. I'll be coming to see you performing at the Skegness Pavilion or something!"

"Ah, no chance. Too scared of big crowds. Just happy to entertain friends and family. Here all summer for your delight!" He took a bow, as his dad laughed again.

They finished off their food and drink, depositing the bag and empty polystyrene cups into the bin, then continued walking down onto the beach. Dogs of all sizes were running round, chasing each other. Mums were sunbathing or reading, kids were building sandcastles and one poor dad was enthusiastically being buried in the sand by two pre-teenage kids.

"I used to hate it when you and your mum did that. It got really cold once you went down a few layers of sand." Dan shivered with the memory. "I'm glad you grew out of it, son."

"Hey, who said I did? There's a shop over there, looks like it'll sell buckets and spades. Give me a few minutes…"

It was gone five o'clock before they turned into Silver Sands Bay and parked the car at Tall Trees Caravan Park again.

"Oh, I forgot to ring Mum back."

"We'll go back to Skeg next week if you want. You can ring her then."

"Yeah. It won't be anything urgent."

"I doubt it, just gossip as usual. I don't know about you, but I'm worn out now, I wonder how many miles we walked."

"A fair few! The crazy golf was fun, I so nearly beat you. Next time, eh? That fish and chip shop was great though, wasn't it? Even better than The Inn Plaice. Must go there again."

Becki

"Where are we going then, Mum?" Jemima's tone was a midway point between excited and bored, a clever spot to be able to hit precisely. The dog sat upright on her lap, panting and looking out of the car window.

"Well, Jem. It's in Skegness, but I thought we'd avoid the seasidey bit for today. It'll be packed now the sun's out. I think today's destination will please us both actually. The man at the caravan park supermarket said his wife loves going. It's a big outdoor market plus you'll be able to use the famous Skeggy Wi-Fi."

Jemima punched the air. "Yay! Result! About bloody time!"

"I'm not sure what it is you think you're missing out on."

"It's FOMO, Mum. Fear Of Missing Out. It's a well-known thing."

"So, you're missing out on a fear of missing out? I'm baffled now. Modern life. Sometimes it's just too much and too fast for me."

"Oh, Mum, you're just getting old, admit it!"

"Cheeky mare!" She grinned at her daughter as she parked her car alongside all the others. They left their jackets on the front seats as it was a beautiful day. Warm, sunny but with a gentle breeze.

Suddenly their phones were alive with beeps! They spent a couple of minutes – well, maybe fifteen – checking things on their phones and Becki rang Jack Butler, seeing as he'd left her a voicemail asking how everything was going. She reassured him the caravan was great and asked after his mum's health, while wandering over to a patch of grass for Trudi to do what she needed to do.

Jemima was busy pressing buttons, laughing and squealing as she read all her messages, checked her Instagram and Tik Tok and Snapchat. She finally put her phone in her front jeans pocket, looking satisfied.

"All caught up, Jem?"

"Yep."

"Excellent. Hope you feel much better now. Let's have a wander round this market then. You okay holding the lead?"

"Sure. Pass it here. But you're picking up any dog poo."

"As always…"

The huge car park was one-third parked cars and two-thirds market stalls and there really was something for everyone there. Jemima headed towards a stall selling jewellery and focused in on some long dangly homemade earrings with dragons, butterflies and all sorts of unusual designs on them, while her mum went straight towards the big book stall. Jemima studied all the gorgeous designs, then chose a beautiful set with pale beads leading to a mini dragon in metallic purple.

"I'll have these, please," she said to the stall holder.

"Do you want them in a box, love?"

"No, it's fine, thanks, I'll put them on."

"No problem."

She put the earrings in and admired them in the mirror on the stall. "They really suit you, love," said the stall holder.

"Thanks, I love them."

She turned round to look for her mum, worried she might not be able to find her in the crowds, but she hadn't gone very far. She walked over towards her. "How many books are you buying, Mum?" She could hardly see her under the pile of paperbacks stacked in her arms.

"They're three for five pound and all brand new. Lots of my favourite authors too." She passed them to the young woman minding the stall, who put them in two carrier bags. Becki thanked her and continued talking to Jemima. "I found a couple of Jessica Redland books I haven't read, a Holly Hepburn, a Lisa Jewell, oh I can't remember the others now, but all good and such a bargain! I'm just going to put them in the car, so I don't have to carry them round with me. Here, give me Trudi, I'll get her a drink of water and give her a couple of biscuits. Then I've seen a local produce stall I want to check out. See if they've got any locally made jams and chutneys. I thought we could pick up some nice bread and cheese for tea then."

"Remember to check for animal rennet in the cheese, Mum!"

"Will do."

"Okay, I'm going to look at that clothes stall over there."

"Here!" Becki pushed a twenty-pound note into her hand. "I'll catch you up."

"Ooh, thanks Mum."

She pocketed the money and headed back to the market, her eyes drawn to a gorgeous tie-dye hoody in purples and blues with a slight swirl of yellow through it. It was only fifteen pounds.

"Would you like to try it on?" asked the middle-aged woman in charge. She had the most incredible pale blue hair, wavy and all the way down to her waist. Jemima thought she looked like a mermaid.

"Yes, please." She wished her straight red hair was a bit more interesting. Maybe she would dye it something bright and daring when she was older or try one of those new trendy pastel hair colours. She thought she'd suit lilac. She wasn't sure if they allowed dyed hair in her new secondary school. Probably not. Perhaps she'd use a temporary dye and try it in the Christmas holidays. She pushed the thought of her new school away; she would deal with those fears another time. Meanwhile, she had just spotted another arty-crafty type of stall and wandered off to have a nosey…

Back at Tall Trees Caravan Park, Becki and Jemima took Trudi and their new purchases into the caravan. They had all got something; even the dog had some new meaty treats and a bag of organic dog biscuits. Jemima was wearing her new tie-dye hoody, which her mum had already complimented.

"Dan and Freddie's caravan looked empty when we drove past."

"Oh, I didn't look, which one is it?"

"The brown and white one. Diagonally opposite."

"Ah. They must have had a day out too, maybe?" Becki clicked the kettle on and put the cheese away in the fridge for later and the bread' jam and chutney on the side.

"Aren't you interested in him, Mum?"

"Who?"

"Dan obviously."

"Well, he seemed nice looking, from what I saw of him."

"So?"

"So, nothing. What more is there to say?" She stirred milk into the two teas and brought them into the lounge. "I don't know him; I haven't spoken to him and I've only seen him from a distance." She shrugged.

"It could be that you've found a really good man here."

"What? On a caravan park in Silver Sands Bay?"

"Why not, Mum?"

"Well, if I was going to have a holiday romance, I'd be thinking more exotic. You know, the Canary Islands or somewhere hot. Bikinis, too-short shorts, palm trees, white sand, clear blue sea and cocktails."

"It was twenty degrees today."

"Hmm. Hardly Caribbean temperatures! You know what I mean!"

"Besides, I wasn't thinking a holiday romance. That's a bit, well, not nice. A bit, sort of, cheap and nasty. I was thinking maybe you could find another partner. Long-term, not short-term."

Becki drank her tea and looked out at the sun reflecting its yellow light off the painted sides of other caravans.

"I don't know, Jem. I just don't know…"

"I'd like to see you happy again, Mum."

"It's not that I'm *unhappy*, Jem."

"No, I know but…"

Becki went into the kitchen, ostensibly to tidy up, but as soon as she was out of sight of her daughter, the tears dripped into the sink. She noisily filled it with water and washing-up liquid, composing herself as she washed up the few pots they'd used today.

Dan

Dan was whizzing through his T. M. Logan book and just as well as the weather had turned. At least he had a good way of spending his time, when they were confined to barracks. After a few days of sunshine and temperatures in the early twenties, it was raining again. Well, more than rain, it was absolute cats and dogs out there. He finished the dregs of his second coffee of the morning and looked up as his son walked in, dressing gown wrapped tightly round him, that little bit of hair stuck up in the middle like it usually did after sleeping.

"Sunbathing today then, Dad?"

"Yeah. After you!"

"I found some board games in the cupboard yesterday, you know, when you went for your shower."

"Did you? Oh, I haven't looked in all the cupboards yet."

"Most of them don't have much in. But this one – "He opened the door of the cupboard next to the fireplace, where the table folded away. Dan could see a large, impressive pile of old, faded jigsaw boxes and board games. "It's a treasure trove!"

"Wow! Isn't it? Is that your plan for today then?"

"Considering the monsoon outside, I think it's our only possible course of action."

"Oh, do you, indeed?"

"I do, yes. The only issue is that some of these games are for at least four players."

"Ah. Aren't there any for two? Or some playing cards or something? I could teach you Drawing the Well Dry, I used to play that for hours with Grandad."

"Well, I was thinking…" Freddie was grinning now, in that cheeky way he had. This was usually just before his asked his dad for £4.99 for Roblox, but they knew that wasn't an option here, without any internet. "I was thinking, Dad. We need a couple of other players. Why don't I get dressed, then pop over to see if Becki and Jemima want to come over? The dog too, of course."

"Ah, I see what you're up to, Freddie, son. Hmmm. We'll see. You get dressed – which will probably take until lunchtime – and then maybe the sun will be out, and we can nip into Chapel St Leonards for the day, like we talked about."

Freddie gave him a look. "Oh, go on, Dad, it's not like I'm suggesting you take Becki out on a date. Just that we see if they want to come over and play some board games."

His father stared at the lad, but said nothing, so he continued trying to persuade him. "It's raining over at their caravan too. They'll be just as bored as we will be."

His dad's face was starting to crack into a familiar smile.

"And they can bring their gorgeous, cute, cuddly spaniel!"

He grinned at his son. "My, you are a persistent little sod at times! I give in, I agree. The dog swung it though, not the rather attractive woman of around my age." He winked. "But you still need to get dressed first. You're not going anywhere in your dressing gown."

Freddie ran back into his bedroom to get himself ready.

"And son, remember to brush your hair!"

Becki

It was miserable out. Cold in the caravan, absolutely pissing it down outside. She did enjoy listening to the sound of the drips landing on the aluminium roof, but she'd heard it enough now and wanted it to fine up again. She'd really been hoping for a decent British summer. Just this once when it actually mattered. Nice weather, so she could spend some quality time with her daughter - have some days out, explore the Lincolnshire coast together. Instead, she could foresee the day being one when all Jemima moaned about was the constant rain and the lack of bloody internet. Oh joy.

Just then, she heard a knock at the door. What? Who was going to be knocking on the caravan. They didn't know anyone.

"Mum! Door!"

"I heard. What are you doing?"

"Getting dressed," came the reply from behind the closed door of the single bedroom.

"Okay. I'll go then. At least one of us is decent."

Becki opened the door slowly.

"Hi Becki, how are you?"

"Oh hello. It's Freddie, isn't it? Come in out of the rain." He came in and she shut the door behind him, indicating towards the lounge with her right arm. He headed in that direction but was quickly distracted by a happy little spaniel insisting her tummy was rubbed.

"Do you want a cup of tea? Jemima will be out in a minute."

"Oh, yes please, if it's no trouble?"

"No, I'm due another one myself anyway. What a miserable day!"

"Yes, that's what me and Dad were saying too."

They walked into the lounge, Trudi jumping round his ankles asking for more fuss. The kettle boiled and Becki went back in the kitchen to finish off the teas, just as Jemima came out of the bedroom, fully dressed with her red hair up in a high ponytail and wearing her new hoody from the market.

"Hiya, Freddie, you okay?"

"Yeah, just bored. You?"

"Same."

Becki brought in three cups of tea and put two on the table, passing the third to Freddie, who thanked her and took a sip.

"So, Freddie, what are your plans for this glorious summer's day then?"

"Well, that's what I came round here for really. My Nan and Grandad own the caravan we're staying in, and we've discovered a whole cupboard of board games. Well, there's a load of different things in there really, cards and some puzzles too. So, Dad and I wondered if you both fancied coming over to ours for a few games of whatever is in there? You can bring Trudi too, of course," he added, being greeted by a wagging tail and another lick on his hand.

"Well, the sunbathing looks like it's off for today," replied Becki. "And we didn't have anything else planned. What do you reckon, Jem?"

"Sounds good to me. Is it just the two of you then over there? Is that why haven't you got enough players?"

Becki rolled her eyes.

"Yes, just me and Dad. Mum left a few years ago, so it's just the two of us. Not even a dog."

"That's okay, you can borrow ours!"

"Let's finish these teas, then we'll all go over then."

Dan

As soon as Freddie had left, Dan started to run round the caravan clearing up. Not that it was filthy or anything, but he finished the last bit of washing up and checked the door to the portaloo was shut, spraying a bit of deodorant outside, just in case it whiffed at all. He didn't know quite why he was tidying up; it was only two people he barely knew, coming round to play some old board games after all.

It was about fifteen minutes before he heard voices outside and the caravan door opened, his son dashing in first and making the introductions between Becki and his dad. The dog ran in at the same time, rushing over to him and jumping up his legs until Dan picked her up and gave her some attention. What a beautiful dog she was! "Hello, you, aren't you a beautiful little thing!" he cooed.

"Oh, she'll take all that fuss and more!" laughed Becki, as Dan indicated for them to sit down.

"Tea or coffee?"

"No, thanks, we just had a cuppa back over there, so we're fine for a bit."

"No problem." He brought Trudi into the lounge and set her down on the floor. She immediately ran round the rest of the rooms checking everything out.

"She loves having a nosey round at everything, making sure she's sniffed out every crumb!" Becki looked out the window. "Oh, you can just about see our caravan from yours then. We're hiring it from the Deputy Head at my school." She noticed Dan's puzzled expression. "Oh, I'm a teacher, not the oldest pupil in the world!"

They laughed. "His mum's ill, so it's available for the whole summer."

The rain suddenly came down with even more intensity and they were silenced for a short time, until the noise of the rain banging on the caravan roof quietened slightly. "Oh, I do love that sound, makes you feel all warm and cosy being inside with that weather out there!"

"Yes," agreed Dan. "I loved snuggling down under the blankets as a kid here, listening to the rain beating down above you. There's something quite relaxing and calming about it."

They made small talk for a few minutes, then Dan indicated the pile of board games, packets of playing cards and various vintage jigsaw puzzles they'd taken out of the cupboard.

"So, this is my parents' caravan, so these things are all pretty old, but still with enough life in them."

"A bit like you, Dad!" joked his son.

Dan continued "We used to come here for years, but not since Freddie was born. Erm, my ex, Melanie - Freddie's mum, she wasn't keen on caravans."

"So that's why she's not here now?" Jemima jumped in with the question, receiving a meaningful look from her mother, which was equivalent to be called by her whole name. Dan didn't seem the least bothered though.

"No, we split up years ago. Not only did she not like caravans, it turned out she wasn't too keen on me either!" He tried a laugh, but it didn't quite work.

Perhaps feeling the slightly awkward change in the atmosphere, Becki stood up and started moving the boxes around, seeing what games were on offer. "Oh, 'Sorry!' I loved that game. I played this as a kid with my parents, it was great fun."

"Me too," agreed Dan. "We must be about the same age. Was it a '70s game or an '80s game?"

"Both, I think, I'm not sure exactly."

"If we had a phone signal," moaned Jemima. "We could look it up on Google and find out."

"Ah, the common teenage complaint!" Becki and Dan exchanged sympathetic looks but continued talking. "I'm fifty," she said.

"Forty-eight," replied Dan. "Not far behind you. Do you remember the television series of the same name?"

"Oh yes! Ronnie Corbett. That was hilarious!"

"Language, Timothy!" they both said at the same time, giggling like a pair of schoolkids.

Jemima and Freddie looked at each other bewildered.

"Never mind, kids, before your time. Back in the olden days when we just watched telly and didn't Google everything first. Right, shall we play 'Sorry!' then?"

Freddie shrugged; Jemima was looking at the other board games. "There's Monopoly," she said triumphantly, holding it up. "A real vintage edition, look at the box!"

"That's gorgeous," Becki said. "I think we had a similar version, but not as nice as this one."

"We can play both anyway," suggested Dan. "I don't think the sun's coming out any time soon and I don't know about you two, but Freddie and I haven't got anything planned."

"Sounds good! We're free too, funnily enough."

They decided to play 'Sorry!' first, each of the four choosing the colour of their pieces, while Dan read the instructions out loud to them all, so they got the gist of it before they started.

Three hours later, they'd played two games of 'Sorry!' and a rather long one of Monopoly. They'd drank tea and lemonade and munched on crisps and had laughed out loud at all sorts of things. But now the dog was barking at the caravan door to be let out.

"I think she needs a w-a-l-k," said Becki.

"Well, the rain's eased a bit. Why don't we all go out?" suggested Dan. "You can get Trudi w-a-l-k-e-d and we can go to the chippy, then come back here to eat together. How's that sound?"

Everyone agreed it was a good idea, so they all busied about putting on shoes and coats and attaching Trudi's leather lead to her pink collar.

They took a saunter up to the shops and joined the queue for the chip shop.

"There's always a queue for this place!" observed Dan.

"Yes, we said that the other day, didn't we, Jem?" Jemima nodded. "It must be the most popular meal to eat on seaside holidays though, so they must get lots of repeat business from the tourists."

"Mum, why don't you take Trudi for her walk, and I'll stay here so I can check what food I want."

"Is that okay, Dan? You think you can cope with two eleven-year-olds at once?"

He grinned back at her. "Oh, I think so. After all, they'll be getting fed soon. It's like lions at the zoo. They look all scary, then throw them in a chunk of meat and they're big soft pussycats all over again."

"Well, I won't be eating any chunks of meat, thank you very much!"

"No-one's saying you have to, Jem. Oh yes, my daughter's a newly converted vegetarian."

"Ah, I see. No fish for you then?"

"No, but their chips are cooked in sunflower oil, I asked them the other day."

"Shall I give you some money, Dan?"

"No, don't worry, Becki, it's my treat."

"Are you sure?"

"Of course! You can buy tea the next time!"

"Thanks!" Becki grinned and walked off towards the seafront with Trudi. She'd give her a little run on the beach. She was kind of pleased there was going to be a next time…

As they reached the front of the queue, Jemima saw it was the same woman behind the counter. "Any halloumi yet? Or other vegetarian options?"

"Ah, I remember you," the woman smiled. "No, sorry, only chips and peas. Are you here for long?"

"Yes, we're staying the whole summer, for six weeks."

"Us too," added Freddie.

Dan placed their order and as they stepped out the shop, Becki and Trudi appeared looking a little windswept. "We just went for a little jog along the beach," explained Becki, rather out of breath.

"Unplanned, was it?" asked Dan.

"You could say that, yes! Trudi saw a big dog that took her fancy. Pulled the lead right out my hand! Luckily, it was friendly, and they just did lots of doggy sniffing."

"Thank God for that. Wouldn't want anything to happen to your beautiful dog!"

Becki stood and took a few deep breaths.

"Come on, Mum, let's walk slowly back to the caravan before the food gets cold."

CHAPTER THREE

Becki

"Are we seeing Dan and Freddie again today, Mum?"

"We've seen them every day since the games day, love, they might want a day off!"

"But they're lovely. It's fun going round with them."

Becki had to agree. They had only done the usual kind of things – spent a few hours on the beach, been in both lots of amusement arcades, played some more games back at the dog-friendly bingo, ate meals together in their caravans – but it was so lovely doing everything as a four, instead of just the two of them. In some ways, they felt like a little family, and she loved that aspect of it. She had missed that.

"Are you in there, Mum?" Jemima nudged her with a grin. "Off dreaming again?" She waved a hand in front of her face. "Earth calling Mother, Earth calling Mother."

"Alright, cheeky, I get the message. I was just thinking."

"About Dan?" She made a love heart sign with her hands.

"Ha bloody ha! About the four of us actually."

"Yeah, it's been kinda nice going round with them. Almost like a family unit."

Becki stared at her. "How weird. I was thinking exactly the same thing."

"Great minds…"

"It doesn't feel, somehow, wrong to you?"

"Wrong?"

"Yes. You know the last time we did this kind of thing with someone else, it was with your dad. Shouldn't we keep those memories sacrosanct somehow?"

"But they are! Memories are memories. We're never going to forget Dad and no-one's suggesting we should. But you can't wear your widow status all the time, for the rest of your life."

"Widow status?" Becki shot her a look that was pitched somewhere between hurt and anger.

"You know what I mean, Mum. You're not an old woman of ninety, you're only fifty. You can find someone else, start again."

"Hardly…"

"Well, not start again like having babies and stuff. But you know, find someone else to love."

"But, what if…"

"No. Before you say it, no-one would ever replace Dad, we know that. But surely, you'd like a boyfriend or partner or husband or whatever?"

"A husband! Blimey, that was quick. Shall I set a wedding date for me and Dan? How about tomorrow?"

"Alright, sarky bum! You know what I mean."

"I do. Sorry." Becki gave her daughter a big hug. "And I know you mean well. I'm just not sure, I mean, it's been so long…"

"You're enjoying hanging out with Dan, aren't you?"

"Yes, I said I am. Of course. He's great fun."

"And you're attracted to him?"

She hated the blush she could feel burn the tops of her cheeks. "Well, yes, he's a very handsome man."

"So, see how it goes. Don't stop anything before it starts. Don't put up those walls."

"Honestly, Jem, you sound like you're the parent, not me! When did you get so wise?"

Jemima laughed. "I don't know. Watching the agony aunt on *This Morning* in the school holidays?"

"Well, you're a clever girl anyway. You are right, I do see that. But I have all this – I don't know – guilt, I guess. I still love your dad, I always will and I'm not sure how it would feel to love someone else that way."

"You won't love someone else exactly the same way though, will you? It'll be something different. A new dynamic, a new chemistry. You'd make new memories, find new favourite films to watch together or new restaurants to eat in. All sorts."

Becki sighed. "Yes, I know you're right. It just seems a big step."

"Just give Dan a chance. See how it goes."

"Yeah, you're right, I will do. You know, you're really surprising me at the moment, Jem. You're so good at analysing things, seeing all the layers. I'm well impressed!"

"Ah, like you tell me, I'm not just a pretty face, Mum." She tapped the side of her nose. "Not just a pretty face."

Dan

There was a tap at the door. It was five o'clock and they'd not long been back from a quick restocking trip to the little supermarket next door. It was amazing how fast they went through pop and snacks here. They must both be putting weight on.

It was Jemima. "Oh, hi Jem! You okay?"

"Yeah, good thanks. Mum said do you fancy a chippy tea? She still owes you from last time!"

He laughed. "Well, I haven't got it written up on an I.O.U. anywhere but yes, that'd be lovely if she doesn't mind. How about if you and your mum go to the chippy and I stay here and put the kettle on, do some bread and butter to go with it?"

"Sounds good!"

"Can I go with them, Dad?"

"Don't see why not, Freddie. Do you want to bring Trudi over here so she's not on her own and barking?"

"Yep, will do. You work out what you both want, and I'll go and tell Mum the plan."

Jemima skipped back over to her caravan.

"She's a nice girl, Freddie, isn't she?"

"She is. But her mum's really nice too." He dug his dad in the ribs. "Know what I mean?"

"Oh you! She might not be interested in me that way."

"But she might be too. Don't rule anything out. I quite fancy having a stepmother and stepsister!"

"Blimey, that escalated fast!" They both laughed heartily.

Then Freddie became serious again and looked his dad in the eyes, admittedly from a lower position. "I'd like you to be happy. It's a long time since Mum was with us and not all women can be like her. Becki seems just great!"

"We'll see, son, we'll see. We hardly know her really, remember. Don't get too carried away."

There was another little knock at the door.

"Shush now!" Dan winked at Freddie and opened the door, only to be leapt on by a small furry, waggy, kissy canine. "Hello Trudi!" he managed to squeak, in-between licks.

"Put him down, Trudi!" laughed Becki. "You can tell she loves you!"

Jemima and Freddie exchanged a small smile that neither of their parents spotted.

Becki

They got to The Inn Plaice and joined the queue on the pavement. It was early August now and the evenings were warmer, so it wasn't an unpleasant wait. As they got up to the front and saw it was the usual woman behind the counter, Becki smiled at her and received one in return. She got out her piece of paper and read out what Dan and Freddie wanted, then added her own request for fish, chips and mushy peas. She looked at Jemima, but before her daughter could say anything, the woman said, "Would you like some halloumi with your chips and mushy peas? Fried in sunflower oil, like your chips?"

"Oh wow! You remembered! Thank you so much!"

"Got some in specially for you, love!"

"Thank you! That's so kind of you." Jemima noticed the woman's name badge for the first time. "Jean. Thank you, Jean."

"My pleasure!" She winked. "And you're Jemima!"

"I am. You're right!" she said in surprise.

"I heard your mum calling you it. Lovely name."

They walked back towards Dan's caravan, chatting away about Jean and how kind she was to have bought vegetarian food in especially for Jemima.

"You know, she must have been wearing that name badge all the time, but I never noticed it. I was more focused on how awful it was they didn't do more veggie options."

"Well, now they do – and we know she's called Jean."

"I'll make sure I'm extra nice to her from now on. To make up for probably being a bit rude."

"She obviously didn't take it too personally or she'd have never bought you the halloumi."

Dan

The next morning was warm and bright, the sun streaming through the thin caravan curtains and illuminating the lounge carpet, which Dan admitted did look a little old-fashioned in the light, the print rather faded and worn. He had so many wonderful memories of being here though, the fun he'd had all those decades ago, when he was Freddie's age and younger. The nostalgia this place brought him was priceless. He could almost see his parents here now, his mum fussing around and tidying up or cooking, while his dad took him out. They'd go off on fun trips to the beach or the arcades – "getting out your mum's hair" as Dad would say.

Freddie noisily came out of his bedroom and walked into the lounge in his Mandalorian pyjamas, stretching and yawning. "What time are we meeting Becki and Jem?"

Dan checked his phone. At least the time still worked. "In about an hour so you'd better get ready."

"I'm looking forward to beating Jem at crazy golf!"

"Hmm, I wouldn't be so sure. I bet she'll be good at it. She might give you a run for your money."

"We'll see." Freddie grabbed his wash things and towel and headed out for the shower block in his pyjamas and slippers, his hair all mussed up from sleep.

The five of them, including Trudi, all went out in Dan's car, arriving in Skegness around eleven o'clock. It was a hot morning so Becki had brought suncream and made sure her and Jemima were wearing hats. Being fair-skinned, they had to be careful not to get burnt. They had already agreed to try to stay indoors during the hottest hours of the day.

They headed to the crazy golf first of all, grabbing cold drinks from a kiosk on the way. They all enjoyed the game and it was so pleasant being by the seaside, with lovely weather and everyone seeming happy. You could hear children's laughter everywhere and see adults smiling at their little ones' glee, and couples of all ages holding hands as they walked by the golf course.

At one point, Dan and Becki were at the end of a hole, with Jemima and Freddie at the start of it. They were smiling at their parents. Dan had got a hole in one, but Becki was having problems. Her ball kept missing the hole and circling past it every time. They were shrieking with laughter as Becki's attempts got ever more desperate.

"They get on really well, don't they?" asked Jemima.

"They do. I think he's missed this kind of thing, since Mum left."

"Mum too. She's been, sort of empty since Dad died. Like she doesn't want to enjoy herself without him. But that's such a waste, she's still young."

"They both are."

There was a cheer as Becki's ball finally went into the hole. The kids looked up as Dan gave her an impromptu celebratory hug.

"They look like a couple, don't they?"

Freddie laughed. "They certainly do!"

"Could you cope with me as a stepsister?"

"You know, I could think of worse things!"

"Like big hairy spiders?"

"Or big hairy teachers?"

"Like feeding frozen mice to snakes?"

"Ugh. Yeah, okay, you win!" He lifted off her hat and ruffled her hair underneath.

"Oi!" She grabbed the hat from his hands and plonked it back on her head, but they were both giggling.

Freddie took his shot, the ball going straight through the hole underneath the windmill and out the far side, just missing getting a hole in one.

"Wow, good shot!"

"Thanks!"

Freddie walked to the end and easily potted the ball in one shot on his second go.

A couple of holes later, the kids again found themselves together and out of earshot of their parents.

"I've been thinking…"

"That's good to know, Jem!"

"Ha ha! Cheeky sod. No, I've been thinking about our parents."

"Yeah? What about them?"

"Well, they can't really have any time together to chat, can they? Without us around, I mean. We're too young to be left alone, we don't go to bed early like younger kids would…"

"Yes, good point. This is probably the closest they've come to having 'couple time' since we met!"

"And we can't play crazy golf all day every day."

They laughed again, easy in each other's company.

"So, what were you thinking, Jem? Do you have a plan?" He whispered conspiratorially, even though their parents were well out of earshot.

"I do, as it happens. What we need is a babysitter!"

"A what?"

"Don't sound shocked, Freddie. Let me explain. I have a wonderful, crazy Aunt Lizzie, Mum's sister. Mad as a box of frogs, but in a good way. Her girlfriend's spending the whole of August in Nigeria visiting her family, so I'm pretty sure Aunt Lizzie would be free to have a bit of a holiday in Silver Sands Bay. What do you think?"

"I think you're a scheming little elf…"

She dug him in the ribs and made him squawk.

"Seriously, I think it's a great idea, Jem. What are you going to do, can you ring her?"

"Yes, that's what I thought. While we have that elusive internet access and phone signal. I thought later on, I'll say I'm going to ring Natasha – that's my best friend – but I'll ring Aunt Lizzie instead and see if I can get her on board. Operation Romance!"

"Operation Romance!" They high fived.

"Come on, you two!" Dan's voice came from further along the course. "You're lagging behind, we're on the last hole."

"Okay, Dad. Who's winning?"

"Who do you think?" He winked at them both, as Freddie swung his club and hit the white ball straight through the arch, over the bridge and smoothly into the hole at the far end.

"I think you and your dad have been practising on the sly!"

They went to the chip shop on the seafront for dinner, eating out of the paper on the beach, letting Trudi have a little paddle and a sniff round while they sat down. Becki and Jemima reapplied suncream after finishing their chips and they gave the dog a welcome bowl of water.

"I think we're all going to turn into chips, you know," commented Becki. "I'm starting to crave a roast dinner with a whole heap of different vegetables! And not a chip in sight!"

"I'll have to cook you both something healthy," suggested Dan.

"Yes, Dad's a pretty good cook. We don't get many takeaways at home."

Freddie and Jemima had been checking their phones constantly throughout the trip and were now trying not to get greasy finger marks on the screen. As Trudi wandered off towards a family eating interesting smelling sandwiches, Jemima said "I'll get her. I'm going to ring Natasha, while I can get a signal."

"Okay, love."

"I'll come with you," offered Freddie, standing next to her. They walked across the sand, calling Trudi's name, though it wasn't until she had scrounged a piece of meat from the mum of the family that she finally responded to her name.

"Thanks!" Jemima said to the woman.

"No problem. Cute dog!"

"And she knows it!" laughed Jemima.

Freddie and Jemima kept walking, Trudi staying by their side in-between rounding them up as she always loved doing, running round her little pack, making sure everyone was accounted for.

The dial tone stopped, and her aunt answered the phone. "Aunt Lizzie! Hi! It's Jem. How are you?"

About an hour later, when they were all in the amusement arcades and keeping out of the hot sun, Becki's phone rang. She looked at the screen. "Ooh it's my sister, I'd better answer it." She left the noisy arcade and stood outside under the shelter of its entrance.

Twenty minutes later – Lizzie liked a chat! – Becki went back in, found the others by the Penny Falls (though it was two pence coins these days) and suggested they get a coffee in the café area, so she could talk to them in a quieter area. "Don't worry, it's nothing bad!" she reassured them.

They squeezed round a tiny table in the café, cold lemonades and iced coffees in front of them, Trudi under the table panting slightly. It had been a busy day for her and those little legs had done a lot of walking.

"Well, that was my sister Elizabeth, we always call her Lizzie. We're very close, but she's not much like me in looks or personality. She's larger than life, isn't she, Jem?"

"Oh yes, but in the best possible way."

"Yes, she's an artist so she's incredibly creative, vibrant, bright – in every way – both smart and colourful, also crazy and lovely with a heart of gold."

"Sounds great! I'd like to meet her."

"Well, Dan, that's lucky because she's coming to stay in the caravan for a while."

"Oh wow, that's great, how long for, Mum?"

"We've said we'll see how it goes. Ebele is away visiting her family in Nigeria, as you know." She turned towards Dan and Freddie. "Lizzie lives with Ebele, she's her girlfriend, they've been together about fifteen years now."

Dan nodded. "So, Ebele's away, Lizzie's at a loose end and fancies a holiday on the East Lincolnshire coast? Sunny weather – sometimes, chips, sand and slot machines. What more could anyone ask for?"

"Absolutely! I mean, she lives in London so we don't see enough of her really, with us being 'up north' as she calls it and she's busy with her work and everything, but I've told her she can still paint up here. In fact, the coast might be an inspiration for her."

"You two obviously get on well then?"

"Oh yes, we're very close. She's five years younger than me, so she was annoying when I was a teenager and she was little, but as adults, we've always got on brilliantly. You'll like her. She's a real character!"

"So, when's she coming up?"

"Tomorrow!"

"That's quick!"

"Oh yes, once Lizzie gets an idea in her head, she's on it straight away, no messing about."

Becki

"Where's Aunt Lizzie going to sleep?"

"She can either share the double bed with me or put the sofa cushions down on the lounge floor and sleep on those. Or she could have your bed and you sleep with me, but she might find your bed a bit narrow. We'll sort something out. It's a five-berth caravan, you know!"

"It'll be nice having her here. We haven't seen her for months, apart from video calls. It's not quite the same, is it?"

"No, it'll be good to spend that quality time with her. Everyone's always so busy, it's hard to find a time when we're both free."

"That's worked out well then, with you off work for the summer and Ebele being away in Africa."

"I wonder what Dan will think of her."

"Well, if he's expecting a carbon copy of you, he'll be in for a shock!"

"That's very true, Jem, very true! We're chalk and cheese."

They heard the bright pink Mini before they saw it. Lizzie had bought the car over a decade ago and things kept going wrong with it, but she'd get it patched up and keep driving it. The car was so 'her' that she always said she couldn't imagine driving anything else.

"Here she is!"

Becki, Jemima and an excitable Trudi all skipped out to meet her, exchanging big welcoming, enveloping hugs with a visual assault of bright colours and a cloud of sandalwood and patchouli. One thing you could never say about Lizzie was that she faded into the background.

They helped her in with her bags. Tie-dye cotton holdalls full of clothes, a large patchwork bag full of God-knows-what plus her easel, a variety of canvases, sketch books, boxes of paints and brushes.

"I'm not sure where you're going to put all that, sis!"

"You can store some under my bed, Aunt Lizzie. There's quite a lot of space there. And there's that empty cupboard in the lounge. You can fit quite a lot in there."

"Yeah, I'm sure we'll sort it out. Now is that kettle on, Becks, because I've had a long journey and I'm gasping?"

"We've only got normal tea and coffee though."

"Don't worry, I brought my own supply of herbal and fruit teas." She took a handful out of her handbag – well, technically it was more of a shoulder bag. She didn't do small, delicate handbags. She liked bright, roomy and practical.

"How long did the journey take you?"

"About four hours in the end, it's quite a trek from London all the way up here."

Twenty minutes later, the whirlwind had settled, and they were all sitting in the lounge drinking tea. Trudi was on Lizzie's lap being fussed absent-mindedly with one hand, while Lizzie's other hand was gesticulating around the place.

"This takes me back to childhood holidays, doesn't it you, sis?" She continued without letting her sister reply, so Becki just nodded, grinned and let the flow of words continue. "What's the place like? The beach and everything? Plenty to do? I suppose it's only a village or town, which is why you have to go to Skegness for the crazy golf and whatever else they have there, but I'm sure they have a few things worth checking out."

She paused for a sip of tea and Jemima got in quickly. "Yes, Silver Sands Bay is pretty good, we'll show you round later. How's Ebele getting on with her family? Has she been in contact much, while she's been out there?"

"Oh, really good, yes. Her mum's not been too well, she's in her mid-eighties, Ebele was a surprise baby so her mum's that bit older."

"Nothing wrong with older mums!" interjected Becki.

"Absolutely not! But her mum's not doing great, so Ebele wanted to spend a good chunk of time with her while she has the chance. And she's seeing her other family too, she's got loads of aunts, uncles, cousins, plus most of her siblings are still out there."

"How many has she got, Aunt Lizzie?"

"I think it's eight, might be nine even. They're all still in Nigeria except for her and a sister who moved to America in her twenties."

She got out her mobile phone and clicked it to the gallery setting. "Here you go, she sent me some photos. Have a look through."

As Becki and Jemima oohed and aahed at the beautiful photos Ebele had sent over, there was a tap at the door. "I'll get it," offered Lizzie standing up and walking over. She opened it to find a man and a boy there. "Ah, you must be Dan and Freddie?" They nodded and she let them in. "I've heard about you two, how lovely to meet you!" She enveloped Dan in a big, warm hug then did the same to Freddie before letting them past her and into the lounge. They found spaces on the sofas, Dan sitting next to Becki, Freddie next to Jemima. Trudi looked like she didn't know who to go to first, running round chasing her tail, then deciding to jump up on Dan's lap.

"Hello there, little girl!" he cooed, rubbing her long wavy ears.

"I swear that dog smiles!" laughed Lizzie.

"Oh, she does," agreed Jemima. "And she has definitely taken a shine to Dan!"

"It's a two-way thing," said Dan, moving his mouth to avoid a licky tongue heading for it.

Becki rose to put the kettle on. "Coffee, Dan?"

"Please."

"Freddie?"

"Lemonade please."

As Becki fussed round in the kitchen, Dan and Lizzie were getting acquainted.

"Becki tells me you're an artist, Lizzie?"

"Yes, that's right. Mainly painting, but I do some pottery sometimes, dabble in a few crafts. But yes, art is my job and my passion."

"What things do you like to paint?"

"Ooh I do most things really, a bit of this and that – portraits, abstract, still life, but landscapes are my thing, usually in watercolours, sometimes in oils."

"She even brought a load of easels, paints and stuff with her here," commented Jemima. "She came prepared!"

"Oh, great! Maybe we'll get to see some of your artwork while you're staying here then?"

"I hope so, Dan. I suspect the sea will inspire me, new places usually do, all the different light and colours and textures, different views at different times of the day. What do you do, Dan?"

"I'm an electrician. Self-employed. Not half as interesting as being an artist."

"Useful though. And practical. We all need our electrics working!"

Dan

Dan and Freddie had gone back to their caravan. They had all agreed that Dan, Freddie, Becki and Jemima would go to the new swimming pool that afternoon. It was only about five miles away. Lizzie volunteered to stay in the caravan with Trudi and catch up on some rest after her long car journey. Dan sorted out their swimwear and towels, while they chatted away.

"Lizzie's quite a livewire, isn't she? I mean really lovely, heart of gold, but so different to Becki!"

"Oh yes, Dad, you've definitely got the right sister there!"

"I haven't *got* anyone!"

Freddie blushed at his dad's stern tone. "Sorry, wrong choice of word. But you know what I mean. There's definitely a connection between you and Becki. You could be really good together. Jemima thinks so too – "

"You've been discussing my love life with Jemima?"

"Not in so many words. We just both think you make each other happy, and we'd like to see you together."

"Would you? Oh. Well, I'm thrilled I've got two eleven-year-olds deciding what two adults do with the rest of their lives. Here – "He threw his bag of swimming stuff at him. "Take these and get back to Becki's caravan and we'll have no more of this kind of talk."

It wasn't a long drive, but Dan chatted happily with Becki on the way there and seemed to have calmed down. In the back, Freddie whispered to Jemima "I put my foot in it with Dad."

"Oh?"

"I told him how we would be pleased if they got together." He nodded his head towards the front seats.

"Ah. Wasn't he impressed?"

"He thinks we shouldn't interfere."

"We're not interfering. We're just giving them a nudge in the right direction."

"Yes, we're giving them our expertise, our official seal of approval."

"Exactly."

"Well, hopefully they'll come to the same conclusion by themselves anyway."

"And at least with Aunt Lizzie here, they can have some" – she pitched her whisper even quieter and mouthed the words - "quality time."

Freddie nodded knowingly and they grinned at each other.

The new swimming complex was very impressive. Super Water World was one of the latest attractions on the East coast and had obviously had a lot of money spent on it, though that did reflect in the ticket prices, with Dan and Becki commenting they wouldn't be "coming here too often."

Once they were changed and into the pool area, they were quite awe-struck by how big it all was. There was a section for babies and toddlers to the left, with shallow water and everything geared towards supervised safe play for the little ones. Then on the right, there was a bigger area for more advanced swimmers with slides and flumes set at various heights and colour-coded difficulty levels, each one configurated with different twists and turns.

They headed towards the middle section which seemed to have a bit of everything. There were inflatables, not-so-scary slides, water cannons, a pretty waterfall and a wave machine that went on every half an hour. There were little corners for a sauna area, a jacuzzi for about four people, plus a terrace with a beach area and paddling pool, and a large café with plenty of tables and chairs.

"Wow! Look at all this! Where do we start?" asked Dan.

"Ooh the light's flashing! That means the waves are coming, Dad. Let's stay here for now."

The waves started and the four of them enjoyed playing in the water, laughing as the waves started off small then increased in intensity. Afterwards, Jemima and Freddie went off to the medium difficulty slides, their parents waiting at the bottom for them, but it was all fine and they came out waving, not drowning.

Becki and Jemima decided to try out the delights of the sauna and the jacuzzi next, while Dan agreed to go on one of the slightly scary-looking log flume rides with Freddie. As the girls walked into the sauna area, the temperature became noticeably warmer. They sank down into the bubbles of the jacuzzi and Becki sighed with pleasure.

"Oh, this is the life. I could sit in here for hours, relaxing in the warm water. Preferably with a gin and tonic with ice and lemon."

"I think it's an alcohol-free pool, but otherwise, yep, that works."

They lie back for a few minutes, their eyes closed, letting the warm froth wash over them.

"Mum?"

"Yeah?"

"I think Dan's lovely."

"He is, yes. Very nice."

"I mean... have you thought you could maybe, well, have a relationship at all? I mean, like, a proper relationship, not a holiday romance, but, like, long term."

Becki suddenly opened her eyes wide and sat up in the water. "Wow! Have you been thinking a lot about this? You keep mentioning it. All the bloody time, in fact."

"Yes, I have. I know it's not really my business and I'm only eleven and all that, but, well…" Becki was shocked to see tears coming from her daughter's eyes. "I just want you to be happy, Mum. I know we lost Dad and we're never going to forget him or stop loving him, but he's not here and Dan is, and I really think he could make you happy. I think I'd be happier too, because I miss Dad all the time like you do and I know Dan isn't the same as my father, but I love being with him and Freddie. It's different to when there's just us two…"

"Oh, baby!" She gave Jemima a big hug and that was how Dan and Freddie found them, when they walked over a couple of minutes later.

"You both okay?" Dan asked with concern in his voice.

"Yes, we're fine," Becki replied, giving him a look which said not to ask. "How was the log flume?"

"Oh, really fun, you should try it. It's not too fast or scary."

"Yes, we will do, won't we, Jem? Shall we grab a coffee and some pop at the café first?"

"That's a good idea, we'll do that." Dan and Freddie headed for the café area, Becki and Jemima not far behind them. Becki squeezed her daughter's shoulder. "Don't worry, Jem. We'll talk about it later. I appreciate what you said, it took a lot of guts to be that honest." She gave her a quick kiss on the cheek, and they joined the queue for the café.

Becki

They were exhausted by the time they got back to their caravans, but they'd had a lovely day out. As Becki opened the caravan door, she was greeted by a gorgeous aroma coming from the tiny kitchen. As they stepped in, they could see a pan on each of the four rings on the hob and Lizzie stirring things, adding in spices, and singing happily to herself.

"Wow! That smells delicious, sis!"

"It's veggie korma, my own recipe. Ebele loves it, so hopefully you two will."

"You remembered I was veggie, Aunt Lizzie!"

"I did, but Ebele and I mainly eat vegetarian anyway. A bit of fish, but no meat."

"Well, if it tastes as good as it smells…"

"Go and sit down then, it's nearly ready."

"You must have found the local mini supermarket then?"

"I did, yes. I was quite impressed with how much it stocked actually. I got everything I needed. I took Trudi out for a long walk earlier to get my bearings."

"Oh, where did you go?"

"Up on the seafront and along, down to the boating lake, once round the whole lake then back again."

"Well, no wonder she's not bouncing around so much then, poor dog's exhausted!"

Trudi had just jumped up onto the sofa near Jemima and was happily accepting a tummy rub.

"Yes, she's worn out her little legs. Bit like me!" Lizzie guffawed. She had the best laugh, both a bit dirty and very infectious at the same time.

As she dished up the food and then sat round the little table, Lizzie looked at them both. "Now, while you're eating this wonderful meal, you can tell me all about your day. I want all the gossip! Don't leave anything out. I want all the gory details. Jemima, tell me everything they've got at Super Water World. And Becki, I expect you to tell me all about that handsome fella of yours too. No, don't deny it! I can see it in both of you, clear as day. You fancy him, he fancies you and I truly think the situation has promise. Plus, he seems a really good bloke. So, spill the beans, big sis!"

"Do you know, you two," said Becki, looking from her sister to her daughter and back again. "Sometimes I feel rather ganged up on." But she was smiling broadly, nonetheless.

Dan

Dan and Freddie sat down to eat their Pot Noodles, the BBC News on the TV in the background. "Food of the Gods, this!" commented Freddie.

"Well, it'll do for now. We ended up having quite a big lunch in the end, didn't we?"

"Yes, that was a nice place you found. It was a good idea to stop there on the way back."

"It was a fun day all round!"

"It really was! Super Water World was amazing!"

They slurped a few mouthfuls, the inevitable stray noodle escaping down a chin and onto a previously clean T-shirt. Luckily, they had found the launderette on site. Dan cleared his throat and looked straight into the eyes of the son he adored.

"Look, Freddie, I was out of order this morning, having a go at you like that. I'm really sorry."

"That's okay," he mumbled.

"No, it wasn't okay. You didn't deserve that reaction. It just took me aback, that's all. But well, I had a bit of time to think about it today, in-between all the slides and waves and log flumes, and I think you're right, son. I've been held back too long, thinking every woman's just out to use me. But you're right, I don't think Becki's like that at all."

"She's not, Dad, she really is completely different to Mum."

"Yes, I can see that. Looking at the four of us today, it was all so easy and relaxing, no stress, no conflict or arguments. Just really good fun."

"It felt like a family, didn't it?"

"It really did. A good old-fashioned family day out."

They ate a few more mouthfuls, then Dan added: "So I'll think about what you said and maybe try to have a conversation with Becki sometime, just the two of us, see what her feelings are about the whole thing."

"She fancies you too, Dad. Jem told me."

"Bloody hell! Is there anything that gets past you two kids?" He dug him playfully in the ribs, a swirly, slippery noodle dropping to the floor.

"Careful, Dad, that's quality food you're wasting!"

CHAPTER FOUR

Becki

Lizzie had only been staying in the caravan for three days, but in the best possible way, it was hard to remember what it had been like before she arrived. It was amazing to spend such an amount of time together without interruptions from work and the boring daily stuff that usually got in the way. Not only was Lizzie great at cooking, but she helped with everything else too – cleaning, dog walking, picking up bits from the shops, entertaining Jemima while Becki went to the shower block. But then, she should have expected that. She remembered what an absolute rock she'd been when Rob had died five years ago. She had been such a big support to her.

She was also really easy to talk to and they'd had a good heart-to-heart the previous night, chatting in the double bed until the early hours. Her little sister thought the same as her daughter did – that Dan was worth the risk; that he was a decent guy who genuinely cared for her. Lizzie explained what joy Ebele brought to her life and reiterated Jemima's view that she didn't want to see Becki growing older, all alone in that house.

This morning, Becki's body clock didn't let her have a lie-in, so she was up, in the lounge, nursing a coffee at half past seven while Jemima and Lizzie slept on. Trudi had got up for her breakfast and a quick wee in the grass, then realising Becki wasn't planning on doing anything exciting, she'd gone back into the bedroom and snuggled down under the duvet, next to Lizzie's warm body.

Becki looked out the window, appreciating the quiet out there. She couldn't hear any kids playing or any traffic, only some birdsong from the trees on the edge of the site. The sun was out, but still weak, and the air was calm and still, without even a gentle breeze. It felt like she was the only person awake in the world.

The good thing about this was that she had time and opportunity to think. The bad thing about this was, well, that she had time and opportunity to think! She thought she had been dealing pretty well with Rob's death all these years, but she had only been hiding her feelings, not facing them. She couldn't believe her clever, oh-so-grown-up daughter had sussed this out before she had. But Jem was right, as Lizzie had told her during last night's long conversation.

Admittedly, this kind of situation had never come up before. She couldn't think of one instance since Rob died where she had eyed up another man or thought what it would be like to kiss someone else. Well, only Idris Elba and that was different, he was famous so didn't count. But Dan had brought all these feelings bubbling up again. Even sexual attraction and desire, she thought guiltily. But then she pressed that guilt back down. She had to get used to doing that now. She needed to feel absolutely no guilt. She was doing nothing wrong. She was widowed, her husband was dead. She could not be accused of cheating on Rob and as much as she hated to admit it, she knew he had gone. He wasn't coming back.

No, it was time to move on. And if things didn't work out with Dan, then she'd deal with it. But she owed it to herself, to Dan and to Jemima, to give the relationship a fair chance. If she cocked up this opportunity and another one never appeared, she would have missed out on what could be – well, she had to admit it – love. She had only ever loved one man in her fifty years, but she realised these feelings she had for Dan were similar to how she felt in the early stages of dating Rob. Her and Dan could actually become something special. She just had to get used to opening up all her emotions again, after caging them up for so long.

As she sipped her coffee, she kept looking outside and appreciating the stillness. Suddenly, a cabbage white butterfly landed on the outside of the caravan window she was leaning against. She put her hand on the glass and the butterfly shimmied its wings at her before flying off.

Dan

"So, Freddie, you're okay going over to Becki's later and staying with Lizzie and Jem for a bit?"

"Course, Dad, it'll be fun. You know I get on great with Jem anyway and well, Lizzie's a right scream!"

"And you don't mind me and Becki nipping out to the club for an hour or two?"

Freddie laughed. "Dad! I've been trying to get you two together for ages. You're the last one to realise how amazing you'd be together!"

"Yeah, alright, son. Just checking. Didn't want you to think I'd abandoned you!"

"Abandon away! Lizzie said she's going to get some of her painting stuff out for us to have a go at. I'm looking forward to it. You never know, I could be the next Vincent Van Gogh."

"Just don't do anything silly to your ears, son."

Dan hadn't brought many smart clothes with him on holiday, as he hadn't expected to do much more than go round Silver Sands Bay in a T-shirt and shorts. He certainly hadn't brought a tie or suit jacket with him. Never mind. He thought he looked okay in his light blue shirt and black jeans. He'd had a shave but left a bit of designer stubble he'd been cultivating. He was just admiring it in the little mirror in his bedroom when Freddie came in.

"Ooh Dad, looking smart!"

Dan turned to face him and grinned.

"I'll leave you to finish shaving though. You've missed a bit."

He picked up Becki from her caravan, thinking how beautiful she looked. She was wearing a pretty sundress in a pale-yellow floral print and yellow sandals, her long blonde hair hanging loose, and it was the first time he had noticed her wearing make-up. Not too much, but enough to enhance her blue eyes and pale skin. He realised his heart was beating fast and he felt a bit clammy on his forehead and down his back. He was nervous! Mind you, as he hadn't been on a date since he first got with Melanie twenty-odd years ago, he supposed it was a completely normal reaction. It took him by surprise though.

The club over the road had advertised they had a female singer performing that night, so they had decided to go there for the evening to check out the live entertainment. It certainly seemed a bit more of a traditional dating venue than offering to take her to prize bingo or challenge her to a game of air hockey. They got their drinks – white wine for her, a pint of beer for him – and settled at a table in a corner the furthest away from the stage. They wanted to be able to talk, without being deafened by sitting too near the oversized speakers.

They settled into their seats and looked around. The place seemed to have a pleasant atmosphere and a wide mix of customers, from those just old enough to drink to those barely able to walk without a frame. They chatted about nothing major for the first half an hour, both feeling a bit awkward. They talked about the kids (always a safe subject), Lizzie, Trudi and Silver Sands Bay itself.

Another drink was bought, and the singer was introduced. They didn't catch her full name – Julie something – but she was in her thirties, quite plainly dressed and with her long brown hair covering her face slightly as she sat on the stool and raised her guitar. But while her appearance was nothing flashy, her singing was beautiful. She sang a couple of familiar cover versions they knew and then introduced a few songs she had composed herself.

"She's quite like Eva Cassidy, isn't she?"

Becki nodded. "Yes. Beautiful voice."

They applauded enthusiastically after the forty-minute set. Julie what's-her-name truly had a stunning voice and was very talented, but obviously shy too. She barely lifted her head to smile at the audience, then gave a little bow and disappeared off into the curtains at the side of the stage.

After she had finished singing, many of the customers left the club, having seen what they came for. A few were obviously locals, shouting goodnight to the bar staff by name, but there were lots of tourists there too.

"You okay for another drink, Becki?"

"Yes. I am if you are. I'm sure our little angels will be happy enough with my sister."

"Oh yes. She had promised Freddie she'd let him have a go with her paints, so he was really excited."

"Yes, she told me she was going to see if the kids fancied a quick art lesson."

Dan went up to the bar to get the drinks.

Becki

Becki was having a really lovely evening. It was so easy to be in Dan's company. But she knew they needed to have a talk, while they had this rare time together without anyone else listening in. They'd only known each other a little over two weeks, but she wanted to ask him some questions, check he was on the same page. It was okay Lizzie and Jemima assuring her he felt the same, but what if he didn't? That would be really embarrassing. She needed to know where she stood. This felt so alien to her. She could feel her heartbeat increasing as he headed back towards the table, two glasses and two packets of crisps in his hands.

"I thought you might fancy a snack."

"Ooh thanks, my favourite brand and flavour!"

"Oh. Mine too!"

They sipped their wine and beer for a while, the silence becoming a bit uncomfortable, when Becki sighed inwardly, composed herself and said, "I suppose we should talk about 'us' while we have the chance."

"I suppose we should."

There was another pause, which they both broke by laughing out loud at the same time.

"It sounds like a board meeting!" she giggled.

"Maybe we need a secretary to take notes?"

Dan's arm slipped and he nearly dropped his pint, Becki putting her hand out to catch it, just as his hand did the same and landed on hers. They stopped laughing and looked deep into each other's eyes. Without even realising what they were doing, their lips met, and they began kissing. It was only a cheeky wolf whistle of some unseen customer that broke the spell.

They both returned to sipping their drinks. Dan opened a packet of crisps and offered her one. "This is just like being sixteen again!" he sighed. "I can't believe I feel so… well, unsure, I guess."

"Yes, it's like being sixteen, but with wrinkles and stretch marks." Becki finished her wine with one last big drink. "I can't believe how nervous I feel."

"Me too. But that kiss was amazing, Becks. I've wanted to do that since we first met here."

"It was rather lovely," she smiled at him shyly.

Dan finished his beer and plonked his glass next to hers. "I think we need one more round, don't you?"

She put her hand on his. "Yes, but first, there's something I need to do…"

She reached across, put her arm round his shoulders and her lips moved towards his.

Lizzie

What fun they'd all been having! It had been like teaching again, she had loved it! Jemima and Freddie both thought it was super exciting to be doing an art class with "a real artist" and had lapped up everything she'd said. She had given them a few pages out of her sketch books and they'd tried a pencil sketch each, then had applied colour using her cheaper paints and brushes that she used to practice her ideas with.

Both Freddie and Jem had decided to try drawing Trudi, then painting her after. She was helpfully fast asleep on one side of the sofa. They really hadn't done a bad job at getting her likeness; Lizzie was impressed with both their enthusiasm and their potential.

As it ticked round to ten o'clock and the kids were finishing off their paintings, Lizzie wondered how things were going over in the club. She knew how much of a big deal this was for her sister. She'd been there with her when Rob died and had stayed with Becki and Jemima for several weeks afterwards. Although her big sis seemed to be dealing with everything quite well now, she knew it had been a hard fight to keep going and that a part of her had been irrevocably broken when her husband had breathed his last breath. She was proud of Becki for even considering a new relationship but knew it would be the best thing for her in the long run – and for Jemima, who was missing out on a father figure too.

"What do you think, Aunt Lizzie?"

Lizzie turned her attention back to their artwork. "I think they're both great. You've really got her expressive eyes perfectly captured and Freddie, your colours are spot on. I think a few more sessions and you could both become pretty good artists. You could maybe even end up doing Art as one of your GCSEs in the future?"

"Ooh that would be great! It's very therapeutic too and relaxing. And your art lessons are much more fun than the ones at school."

"Ah thanks, Jem. Yes, art is my go-to in all sorts of stressful situations. Very good for your wellbeing and mental health. Maybe one day while I'm here, we can go to the beach and do some painting there, if we find a day that's not too windy. You don't want to be chasing your sheets of paper around the sand! Believe me, I've been there! Anyway, we ought to pack up now and get the caravan tidy again. I shouldn't think it'll be too long before your parents are back from the club."

"I hope they've been having a nice time," commented Jemima.

"I hope they have used the time to talk!" laughed Freddie. "Not just drinking alcohol and chatting about the weather!"

"Fingers crossed, kids, fingers crossed!"

Becki

They walked slightly unsteadily back to the caravan, chatting and giggling – and not just due to the amount of alcohol they'd consumed over the evening. As Becki opened the door, she stepped into the lounge to see three smiling (if slightly painty) faces and a big wagging tail.

"Hi there, you lot! How's your evening been?"

"Mum!" Jemima jumped up. "You're holding hands!"

Becki did a look of mock surprise, peering down at their intertwined hands as if seeing them for the first time. "Oh my God! How did that happen?"

"I think it was that seventh double vodka," teased Dan, swinging their hands forwards and backwards like little children.

Jemima was looking shocked, like she was just about to say something. Becki put her hands up. "It's okay, Jem, I didn't have any vodkas, just a few glasses of wine."

Her daughter relaxed. Freddie and his dad were exchanging happy glances. Lizzie thought it a good time to change the subject, before it all got too intense. "Look at Jem and Freddie's masterpieces!" She indicated the paintings of Trudi drying on the windowsill. "Wow, kids, they're amazing!" Becki moved nearer towards them, picking up one then the other, with Dan peering over her shoulder.

"They really are!" he agreed. "You both look like you're got talent there."

"Aunt Lizzie said so too. She said she'll take us painting on the beach one day this holiday."

"Blimey, sis, you'll be setting up a summer art school before you know it!"

"Well, it wouldn't be my first."

"No, but you've had a few years off."

"Both Jem and Freddie did really well. You should both be very proud of them. Now, do you want a quick tea or coffee?"

"Yes please, coffee for me."

"Won't that keep you awake, Dan?"

"Not me! I have super caffeine resistance built into my system from many years of over-indulgence. Plus, I could do with counteracting the beer somewhat."

Lizzie went to put the kettle on, as the kids excitedly chattered to their parents about their evening painting.

Afterwards, they said their goodbyes, Dan and Becki exchanging a fairly quick kiss on the lips – much to their children's embarrassment – and the guys returned to their own caravan.

An hour or so later, Jemima was in her bedroom asleep, leaving Becki alone with her sister to talk through the evening she'd had.

"So, how was your first date for fifty-seven years then?"

"Ha bloody ha! I'm not that old." She sipped the herbal tea Lizzie had made her, her sister assuring her it would help her relax and sleep after such an exciting evening out. "You know, it was an absolutely lovely night. Thanks so much for babysitting. The place was nice, everyone was friendly, oh and the singer had the most beautiful voice – "

"Yeah, come on, get to the interesting bit, sis!"

"Oh, Lizzie, you have absolutely no patience!"

"Did you talk? Well, obviously you talked. But did you talk about important, relationship stuff? Well, I guess you must have done, because you were holding hands when you came in and then there was that farewell kiss."

"If you ever shut up long enough, I'll tell you!" She threw a cushion at Lizzie, who guffawed and threw it right back. Trudi woke up and jumped down onto the carpet.

"Oh, sorry Trudi, we're not playing, it's bedtime."

Trudi made a kind of sighing noise and trotted off to the empty double bed, spreading herself out right down the middle and going straight to sleep. She didn't need a herbal tea to wind down.

"So, yes, we talked, though it took a while before we built up the courage. And a few drinks. We were both really nervous, unused to dating and all that lovey-dovey stuff. But well, yes, you're right, we do like each other…"

"Like each other? Oh for pity's sake, you like the woman in the chip shop you were telling me about, but you don't want to sleep with her. I'm sure you and Dan more than like each other."

"Well, yes, okay, we're attracted to each other or however you want to describe it."

"So, you're dating? An item? Whatever the youngsters call it nowadays. Courting? Stepping out? Seeing each other?"

"None of them. All of them. I don't know. But, well, we kissed, so yes, I suppose we're something…"

"Kissed as in giving your mate a hug and a peck or a full-on snog-yer-face-off?"

"Don't ever write a romance novel, Lizzie, your way with words needs some working on. But yes, a snoggy snogging snog kind of kiss."

"And?" She dug her little sister in the ribs, noting the colour rising in her cheeks.

"And it was pretty amazing, thank you very much."

"So you didn't nip behind the back of the pub and – "

"No, I bloody didn't! Christ!"

"Sorry, just teasing. I know that's not your style."

"Indeed it isn't! Give me some credit!"

"But, if you'd like to, maybe, spend a little couple time at his caravan one day and you need someone to give the kids another art lesson at all…"

"Hmmm. Let's not run before we can walk, eh? Yes, I'll let you know. Come on, let's go and get some sleep. I'm shattered."

"That's what happens when you get back into the old snogging."

She shut up when a cushion hit her face and they went to bed giggling like they had done when they shared a childhood bedroom all those years ago.

Dan

"How did it go then?" asked Freddie when they got back to their own caravan.

"Really good, son. Becki is lovely. I'm pleased she feels the same way about me as I do about her. That's a big relief!"

"It was pretty obvious, Dad! Jem and I could see it a mile away."

"Well, you were more confident than I was then. Mind you, it's so long since I've been in the old dating game, I've forgotten how to read the signals. But it's a big relief that we got to talk about everything and know where we are. Anyway, you enjoyed being with Lizzie then? She seems a lot of fun!"

"Oh, she is. It was great. We had a wonderful art lesson. Trudi was perfect, she just slept the whole time we were sketching her, then we just needed to paint the colours over the pencil lines. She made it much more interesting than the Art lessons we have at school."

"Sounds like we both had a good evening then." He went to put the kettle on. "So, you wouldn't mind if Becki became my new girlfriend?"

"No, of course not. And before you ask, I'd be happy with Jem being my stepsister too. We get on really well and have loads in common."

"Hang on! We're not getting married yet!"

"No, I know, but anyway, I'm in favour. Overall, like."

Dan brought the teas through. "We'd better go to bed after this. It's quite late."

"Becki and Jem don't live far away from us, do they? When we're home, I mean?"

"No, they're at Harrogate, it's about a twenty-minute drive from our house, so it wouldn't be a long distance relationship or anything."

"That's good. It'd be hard work if she was up in Scotland or down in Portsmouth or something."

"Ah, you remember those epic journeys from our holidays! That was a while ago too."

"I really do. All those hours in the car definitely made an impact. And because you and Mum were arguing back then, they seemed even longer."

"Yes, those were the last two holidays we had together. Sorry about all the arguing you had to put up with, it wasn't fair you had to listen to everything."

"It doesn't matter. It was mainly Mum anyway. I remember thinking that at the time. 'Shut up, Mum, just let's enjoy the holiday,' I was saying in my head. And I'd have only been six, ha ha, but I remember it clearly."

"How funny!"

"It's much better without her, you know, in so many ways. I mean, there aren't many arguments these days."

"Well, only if you leave your dirty washing everywhere or forget to tell me your P.E. kit needs washing. But yes, mainly we get on fine. All boys together, eh?"

"That might change soon, Dad. Add a couple of females into the mix. Three if you include the dog."

"Come on, Freddie, I think it's definitely time for bed now!"

Becki

"Dan and I thought we'd have a day on the beach today, if you fancy it? Well, maybe a morning, then go to the boating lake. Or vice versa. Depending on the weather."

"Yeah, sounds good," replied Jemima.

"All good for me too, but I think it's going to be a bit windy for painting. I'll do that another day. Plenty of time for all that. We've got about three weeks left of the holiday, I think, if I decide to stay as long as you guys."

"What time are we meeting them?"

"In about half an hour."

"Oh okay, I'll have a shower when we get back then. I'll take my swimming stuff in case we have chance for a swim."

"Okay, Jem, that makes sense."

They met up with Dan and Freddie at the agreed time and the five humans and one dog headed up the street towards the seafront.

"Can we go to the boating lake first?" asked Jemima. "Because if we go to the beach and I go swimming, I'll want to go back and change into dry clothes afterwards."

Everyone said that was fine, so they headed off to the left past the café and walked along in the direction of the boating lake. Trudi was happy to find other dogs to sniff as they went along, and all the people they met seemed happy as well. The temperature was already up to twenty-two degrees and the bright blue sky and warm sunshine was raising everyone's mood.

The café was busy when they arrived, so they decided to walk round and look at everything else. It was too early for dinner yet anyway. There were a couple of quite tacky souvenir shops, which Dan and the kids looked round, while Lizzie and Becki stayed outside with the dog. Jemima came out with some seaside rock for her best mate Natasha and some souvenir picture postcards. "I thought I'd send one to Grandma and Grandad."

"Oh, that's a good idea, Jem, they'd appreciate that. People don't seem to send postcards from their holidays anymore. It's a shame. I used to like writing and receiving them."

"These days, Mum, we just message our mates and send them photos of our holiday, while we're away. But we can't here, because…"

"There's no bloody internet!" Becki and Dan said in unison.

Next the kids went on the big Astroglide slide a few times, after deciding that was still okay for eleven-year-olds but they were definitely too old for the bouncy castle. Then they all started to walk around the boating lake. "Shall we go on the Pedalos?"

"I'll hold the dog," offered Lizzie as the other four got in two boats. "It's not something I fancy trying my hand at."

Dan was in a boat with Freddie, Becki in another with Jemima. It was rather relaxing, feet going on the pedals, slowly steering through the calm water of the manmade lake. When they finished their turns and the man who owned the boats helped them out, they couldn't see Lizzie and Trudi anywhere. They headed in the direction of the café though and there they were, Lizzie waiting for them with a bright red Kiss Me Quick hat shoved on top of her bright red hair.

"What do you think?" she asked, pouting comically as she saw them coming towards her.

"I think we'll skip the snogging, thanks," laughed Becki.

"Very fetching!" Dan commented, blowing a kiss in her direction.

"Are you ready for some food yet?" asked Lizzie. "I've been hovering around this table, in case there's a rush on."

"Yes, I think we've all worked up an appetite now."

"My legs are aching," moaned Jemima.

"Oh, you old crock! And that was gentle pedalling too!"

Becki, Dan and Freddie went inside the café, while the others sat down at the table. "Mum, can you get me a cheese salad sandwich or a jacket potato with cheese and beans? Oh, and a Coke, please."

"It's getting a bit colder now, Jem. It was lovely when we got here. Not sure where that sun went to."

"Behind a cloud, I think. Maybe today won't be the day I swim the Channel then." They laughed easily together.

Lizzie got a multi-coloured cardigan out of her bag and put it on, shivering. "Wind's getting up."

"It'll be even worse if I have the baked beans, Aunt Lizzie!"

"Not to worry," Dan came out holding a tray. "No jacket potatoes, so we're spared. Here's your cheese salad sandwich and your Coke. Here's your things too, Lizzie. I'll just go back for mine."

Forty-five minutes later, they had all eaten and drank their fill and were ready to go back. The sky had got much darker and the wind had drops of cold rain deep within it.

"No swimming today then, Jem."

"No, I agree, but can we go up to the seafront to take some pics? I bet the waves look impressive."

"Well, I suppose we could cut up through that path and walk back along the seafront?"

Trudi enjoyed scampering up the path ahead of them, but once they were up on the seafront, Becki put her lead back on. The weather conditions weren't nice at all and she didn't want the dog running off again.

Jemima had got her phone out and was taking photos of the waves crashing down, the blackening sky giving it a rather menacing backdrop. "I'm just going over to that corner bit. There's no railings there, so I can get some better photos."

"Okay, Jem, just be careful."

The rest of them stayed back where they were, looking out at the sea, as the last few people on the beach began racing home to their caravans before it poured down. Jemima was posing for a selfie, her back turned towards the pounding waves. The sea was getting higher, the edges of the biggest waves now biting at her ankles as she leaned backwards to get the best photo, grinning at the camera.

Lizzie had just pointed out some interesting looking birds flying by, when there was a crash behind them and a terrifying scream.

"Jem!" yelled Becki as they all ran over to where she'd been standing. They could see her in the water, her head appearing and disappearing as the waves got higher and fiercer.

Freddie ran off in the direction of the lifebuoy he'd noticed on the sea wall not far away, but as the women looked round to see where he was going, they heard another splash and turned back to see Dan in the water too. He'd jumped in fully clothed and was swimming the short distance towards Jemima.

The sky darkened again, and the rain came fast, hard drops splashing them, soaking their clothes in a couple of minutes. Not that Lizzie or Becki noticed; their attention was solely on the water and what was happening in the sea.

Freddie reappeared and threw the lifebuoy across to his dad who caught it. He lifted Jemima up and put it over her head, then swam with her until they could get out of the water and onto the sand. Becki ran down and the two of them dragged Jemima up the rest of the beach, out of the way of the encroaching waves. As she lay unconscious on the seafront, a young woman ran up. "I'm a nurse, I can help, let me see her."

She turned Jemima onto her side and suddenly, she choked up a load of sea water. The nurse checked her over. "She's okay, she had a lucky escape. That sea can be lethal." Jemima continued to cough and splutter as her mum hugged her tight. "You need to get her checked out though, as she lost consciousness for a bit. Do you know where the nearest hospital is?"

"Yes," Dan answered. "I've seen a sign for it."

"Me too. I know where you mean. I'll take her," Becki replied. "You're soaked through."

"Go and get the car then, we'll stay with her until you get back."

"Bring some blankets too and a change of clothes for her," added the nurse. "You'll need to try and keep her warm."

Jemima was feeling a bit better now and her breathing was almost back to normal. "That'll save me needing that shower!" she joked with Lizzie. Suddenly she realised her hands and pockets were empty and wailed "Oh no! My phone! It's in the sea!"

"It doesn't matter, Jem," teased Freddie. "There's no bloody Wi-Fi anyway!"

Dan

Becki and Lizzie had taken Jemima off to the local hospital to get examined, all wrapped up in blankets, with a bag of dry clothes to get changed into. Dan thanked the nurse, then he and Freddie headed back to their caravan, holding Trudi on the lead. She seemed to be the only one unaffected by all the drama. The rain had eased off by now, but they were all wet – Dan more so than Freddie.

"You were so brave, Dad!"

"Never even thought about it, to be honest. Just jumped in. You were very quick-thinking too, throwing us that lifebuoy."

"I hope she'll be okay, Dad."

"I'm sure she will, son. We got to her quickly and thankfully that nurse came over and she didn't seem too worried, or she'd have called an ambulance."

Once inside the caravan, Dan stripped off and got dried and redressed in his bedroom, while Freddie towel-dried the dog then got changed himself.

"I'm not sure if my shoes will recover," Dan said, as he put them into the sink. Not only were they completely soaked through, but the sand had discoloured them and the inner soles had gone missing somewhere in the sea. "At least I've got my trainers in the suitcase. Not that it's important in the grand scheme of things. I can always pop into that market Becki was on about and pick up a new pair. Shoes are trivial. We couldn't have replaced Jemima…"

He heard sobbing and looked up. "Oh Freddie, come here, son." He gave him a big hug. "I know, it's the shock. Don't worry, you were amazing and I'm sure Jem will be absolutely fine."

Three hours later, there was a rat-a-tat-tat on their door. It was Lizzie. On her own. She saw Dan's worried face when he realised it was only her and she put her hand up. "Don't worry, she's fine."

"Come in, Lizzie. Tell us what's happened. Coffee?"

"Go on then, I think I need one after today."

She explained they were keeping Jemima in for observation overnight, but they weren't too worried. The doctor said it was routine to make sure her body temperature was stable and she didn't get hypothermia. Becki was staying there with her.

"Obviously I was surplus to requirements so I offered to come back and update you both and take Trudi home." Lizzie was fussing the dog and got a lick on her nose as she said her name.

"Oh, that's such a relief, we've both been worried and wondering what was happening." Dan said, sighing and relaxing at last. He hadn't realised how tense his shoulders had been until then.

"You were so brave, jumping in the sea like that! You could have been injured or even drowned yourself!"

"It was instinctive, not brave. I said the same to Freddie. I'm quite a strong swimmer so I don't think I would have drowned. I just wanted to get Jemima out of there as soon as possible, that was all I was thinking about. It happened so fast!"

"You were fab too, Freddie, running to get the lifebuoy. Me and Becki were just frozen in fear and you two were off like action men!" Lizzie downed the coffee in a few mouthfuls. "Oh, that hit the spot. Can I make myself another?"

"Of course, be my guest."

She went into the little kitchen and switched the kettle on to boil again, rinsing her cup at the sink. "Oh! Dan! Your shoes! Look at them, they're ruined. We'll have to get you a new pair."

Becki

It was almost midday by the time they got back to Tall Trees Caravan Park. Jemima had passed all her health checks and been released by the hospital, then Becki had driven her back. They'd stopped for a McDonald's on the way to Silver Sands Bay, as Jemima was starving and fancied a veggie burger and fries.

As they were about to open the caravan door, Lizzie got there first and gave her niece a great big bear hug. "How are you doing? Come and sit down."

"We're both tired, Lizzie. Neither of us got much sleep last night."

"But I'm fine, all clear to come home. No hypothermia."

"Well, that's great to hear, Jem. You look exhausted though, both of you. Do you want to go for a nap?"

"Yeah, I will, Aunt Lizzie." She yawned as she walked towards her bedroom, the patter of tiny paws following behind.

"Trudi's missed you!" commented Lizzie.

Once Jemima's door was shut, Lizzie asked "What did they say at the hospital then?"

"Nothing we couldn't have guessed really. She was lucky. Between Dan, Freddie and that nurse, they probably saved her life. I think she's learned her lesson, bless her. No more selfies for her. Well, she's got no phone at the moment anyway."

"You should see Dan's shoes too, they're ruined!"

"Oh bugger, I didn't think about that. Are his clothes okay?"

"I assume so. When I went over yesterday, his shoes were in the sink. I didn't see his clothes. They were probably drying somewhere."

"I'll have to offer to buy him some new shoes."

"Oh, I doubt he'll be too fussed. He wasn't complaining."

Dan

"What time can we go over and see them, Dad?"

They had both seen Becki and Jemima walk up the caravan steps and being enveloped enthusiastically by Lizzie just before the door shut behind them.

"Oh, we'll leave it until later. They'll probably be tired. Hospitals aren't the best places for a good night's kip. Besides, we're off out."

"Are we? Where to?"

"You'll see. Come on, get your shoes on. Ah, that might be a clue!" he added, mysteriously.

Dan drove them to the outdoor market. "Is this the market Becki was talking about?"

"It certainly is. I thought I could get myself some replacement shoes and maybe we'll see if there are any stalls selling mobile phones."

"But you've got a mobile phone."

"Yes, but poor Jemima hasn't. Do you know what brand hers was?"

"Yeah, same as mine, we compared them on Skegness beach and laughed how we had exactly the same model."

"Ah, brilliant. You can tell me what to buy then."

"Can I get something for myself?"

"Well, not a new phone, but yeah, see if anything you see takes your fancy."

An hour later, they were back in the car and heading towards Silver Sands Bay. They'd had a productive trip out and were pleased with their varied selection of purchases. The plan was to wait until about four o'clock, then pop to the chip shop and get everyone some tea, then take the food and their pressies over to Becki's caravan. Hopefully that would cheer them all up, after such a traumatic experience the day before.

Becki

Becki saw Dan and Freddie walking towards the caravan just as the kettle began boiling. "That was good timing," she said as she opened the door. "Did you hear the kettle?"

"No, it must be our sixth sense. Coffee please." Dan bent to give her a quick kiss on the lips. "I've brought tea from the chippy for everyone too."

"Oh thanks, that's really kind of you."

"You remembered I'm veggie?"

"Yes, Jem. Your mate Jean recognised us and asked if we were buying for you too, so she sent you your halloumi."

"Aw, she's such a sweetheart!"

"Jem! You thought she was a right miserable cow when you first saw her."

"I've changed my opinion now. She's fab!"

"Right, I'll dish up the food," offered Lizzie, taking plates, forks and the carrier bag through to the little dining table in the lounge.

"I'll do the hot drinks then," said Becki. "Freddie, do you want a hot drink or a lemonade like Jem?"

"Lemonade please."

"Dan! You've got new shoes!"

"Yes, Lizzie, we've been to the market Becki recommended, they were only fifteen quid."

"Very smart."

"Oh Dan, you should let me pay for them, you shouldn't have to shell out for new ones."

"No, Becki, honestly, it's fine. Anyway, I've got some pressies for you all. You're right, that market is pretty impressive. We both found lots of interesting bits and pieces. We went to the bread and cheese stall you recommended too."

"I loved it," said Jemima. "Loads of different stalls to look at."

They sat down in the lounge and Dan rustled in his bag of goodies. "So, first of all, a pressie for Lizzie!" He handed over a small box which she opened, her eyes widening as she saw the contents.

"Oh my God! They're perfect! Look Jem!"

She handed over the earrings, which were miniature easels with a tiny paint palette on a dangly gold hook.

"Oh wow! Aunt Lizzie, they're so you!"

"That's what we thought," agreed Dan, as Lizzie gave him a big hug and a kiss on the cheek. "Thanks Dan, that's so thoughtful of you."

Next, he took out a pretty pink dog collar with little diamante studs round it. It had a tag on it with TRUDI engraved on it in a curving font. "This is for Trudi, though I thought she'd probably like something to eat too, so I got her a bag of doggy treats as well."

She came over and licked his hand, sniffing the bag eagerly, so he opened it and put a couple on the floor for her.

"Now, I'm going to eat the food before it goes cold, then I'll do the last two presents afterwards. I hate cold chips!"

"Yes, eat up, Dan, we can wait," said Becki, though her daughter gave her a look which said she was feeling rather more impatient than her mum!

The food was all finished and everything had been tidied away, so Lizzie offered to make more drinks while Dan gave his last two presents to Becki and Jemima. Becki opened the little blue box curiously and inside it, she found a silver necklace with an open book at the end. "Is that because I'm easy to read?" she teased.

"It's because of your love of reading." He smiled at her, noticing her pretty blue eyes twinkling in the light.

"Oh look, it's even got a tiny bookmark made out of silver too. It's gorgeous, thank you so much, what a lovely gift!" She kissed Dan on the lips.

"Dad spent ages looking through the book stall but didn't find anything for you."

"Well, I found loads of books I thought you'd like, but I didn't know if you already have them."

"Oh, Mum does that!" laughed Jemima. "She'll often buy herself a book and come home to find she's already got it."

"Yeah, that's true, I own up."

"Right, the final present!" Dan tapped a little drumroll out on the table. "For Jemima…"

He handed over the bag, empty now apart from the one last box. As she looked in, she squealed with excitement, taking it out the bag. "A phone! And just the same as my old one!"

"Now, it is refurbished, Jem," Dan explained. "But the guy on the stall reassured me they are good quality and last well. So, you've obviously lost the things on your phone, but hopefully you can download all the apps again and at least get some things working once you get an internet connection. We'll just need to get you into Skegness town centre at some point. But it's a start!"

"Awww thanks, Dan." Jemima gave him a big cuddle. "That's perfect!"

"But" Dan continued in a serious voice. "No more taking selfies near big waves! Or even small ones. It's not worth the risk."

Jemima nodded solemnly, as her mum said, "And so say all of us!"

"You guys had quite the shopping trip, eh?" Lizzie grinned as she passed round teas and coffees before coming back with a herbal tea for herself and sitting down on a sofa. "I'm the only one who hasn't been round this amazing market. Mind you, it's probably better for my bank account if I stay away from it. Funky jewellery, brightly coloured clothes and a big book stall are just the kind of things I spend far too much money on."

Lizzie

After all the drama, they had a couple of days just pottering around quietly. Jemima's accident had taken its toll on everyone in their own way and they all needed to process it. Lizzie kept going over different scenarios in her head and worrying over what could have happened if it had only been the three of them. She was no good with water, never had been, so she couldn't have jumped in after her niece. Maybe Becki would have done. She needed to stop it all going round and round in her head.

She needed something to distract herself with, someone to talk to who was a bit detached from all that had happened. She offered to take Trudi for a walk, which Becki thanked her for, as she was feeling a bit worn out and had been trying to put it off.

"I might give Ebele a ring from that payphone too, check how they're all doing."

"Good idea. What's the time difference between here and Nigeria?"

"It's the same as here. Sometimes they're an hour ahead, but at the moment, it's the same."

"Oh, that's good then. No need to worry about ringing her in the middle of the night or anything then."

Lizzie took a leisurely stroll past the arcade on the corner and up to the prize bingo, then back to the phone box, chatting to the dog all the time. She planned to ring Ebele then give Trudi a little run on the beach before turning back towards the caravan site.

The telephone box was empty, so she got in, holding Trudi's lead tightly in one hand as she organised her money and the piece of paper with the number on in the other. As with all phone boxes, it had that slight whiff of urine. It seemed to take a while to connect, then a man's voice answered the phone, speaking in a strong African accent.

"Hello! Can I speak to Ebele, please?"

"Hold on, I'll get her for you."

"Thanks." There was a lot of noise in the background, but Lizzie knew Ebele had a large family. She waited a minute or two, then a rather subdued voice answered with a quiet "Hello?"

"Ebele? It's Lizzie. Are you okay? You sound upset."

"Oh Lizzie, it's good to hear your voice. It's been awful."

Lizzie realised her partner was trying to hide her sobs. She could hear the crack in her voice.

"Ebele! What on earth's happened?"

"Mum was getting better, she really was. She was sitting up in bed, eating again. We were all chatting together, laughing – the whole family is here, as you know. Then this morning, she just died. Out of the blue. We were here with her, laughing together and she just died."

Her tears were flowing freely now, and Lizzie could hear a female voice in the background asking if she was okay.

"They think it was her heart in the end. She was so weak…"

The sobs upset Lizzie so much. She couldn't do anything to help. She couldn't even give her a hug. "I'm so sorry, for all of you. I wish I could be there."

"It's okay. Don't worry."

"Shall I ring you tomorrow?"

"I don't know, Lizzie. There's so much to organise. Isn't your mobile working? I sent you a message but it said it wasn't delivered."

"No, I'm at the seaside with Becki and Jemima. Long story, but no internet here or much of a phone signal. It's a bit in the middle of nowhere. I'm calling from a payphone, for God's sake! It's like 1985. Look, I'll give you a couple of days and ring you then, see how things are."

"Okay. I'd better go. My sister needs me."

"Okay, honey. Look after yourself."

There was a click the other end.

"I love you," said Lizzie to the dial tone.

She must have taken Trudi on the beach because her shoes had sand in them when she got back to the caravan, but she couldn't remember doing it. She was reliant on muscle memory by now. Everything felt numb. She wasn't thinking straight. Would Ebele come home soon? Or stay out longer to help her family? Why hadn't she said she loved her? Maybe she'd stay in Africa now her mother was gone. A million theories and situations were racing round her head. It was all too much.

It was pointless trying to work things out now. She just needed to get back to her sister and her niece, have a strong coffee, let her brain sort out things at its own pace. She'd ring Ebele in a few days and hopefully things would be fine between them. It was just the shock and the grief. At least she hoped that was all it was, but deep down, she was terrified it was something else.

Still in a daze, she opened the caravan door, Trudi running in excitedly as if to tell Becki and Jemima all about her walk. Becki looked at her sister and knew something was wrong straight away.

"Sit down, sis, you look awful, what's wrong?"

"I rang Ebele. Her mum died this morning."

CHAPTER FIVE

Dan

Dan had offered to take Jemima out with them, so Becki and Lizzie could spend a quiet day together. Lizzie was in a right state after her telephone call with Ebele and hearing about the death of Ebele's mother. Somehow, it seemed to have rocked Lizzie and made her question if there was even a future for their relationship. Dan didn't know the ins and outs, it wasn't his business, but he had a lot of time for Lizzie and knew she was suffering and needed a bit of sister time with Becki.

He decided to have a bigger drive out and take the two kids to Lincoln. It was a city he'd never visited, but it was only an hour or so away from Silver Sands Bay and there was plenty to do there. He knew there was the beautiful and famous Lincoln Cathedral and the Lincoln Castle and both were near to each other. He parked in a big car park nearby and as the first thing they saw was a café, they went in there for a late breakfast.

It was a lovely café, with comfortable seats and friendly, efficient staff and the prices weren't bad either. Jemima was thrilled to find they did her favourite meal – smashed avocado and poached egg on sourdough toast with tomatoes on the vine. Her enthusiasm was infectious and the three of them ended up ordering the same, though Dan had a coffee and the kids lemonade.

The food really was delicious! Dan and Freddie complimented Jemima's choice and agreed it was up there with their favourite meals too.

"I'll soon be converting you all to vegetarianism!" she teased.

"Well, I do like my fish," said Dan. "Though I hardly eat any red meat, so that would be easy enough to give up."

"I'd miss sausages," Freddie commented, swallowing his last mouthful of toast.

"Ah, but they have loads of different veggie ones now, Freddie. You'd easily find one brand you liked at least."

Dan had been looking on his phone to see what attractions Lincoln had to offer, besides its obvious historical buildings. They had already seen the castle quite close up as they came into the car park and it did look amazing. Dan was a big fan of castles and had visited a large proportion of the ones in England, Wales and Scotland, so he was keen to look round Lincoln Castle too.

The kids had spent less time on their phones than Dan had expected. Perhaps they were weaning themselves off them? "Oh, look! We're right near a museum that sounds fun. The Museum of Lincolnshire Life." He showed them the website on his phone. "Sort of social history, military history, old vehicles…"

"Oh, that sounds good," Jemima agreed, Freddie nodding along happily too.

"Well, as we're right near the castle, shall we look round there first, then go to the museum afterwards? I mean, we've got all day. The museum shuts at four o'clock so we've plenty of time."

The kids agreed, so they crossed over from the car park to the castle. Walking up the ramp, they found the board with the list of prices on. "The medieval wall walk is £10.50 for adults, £5.70 for you two. Do you fancy it?"

"I'm not really bothered, Dad. We can walk through the grounds for free and see most of it."

"I'm scared of heights too," said Jemima. "So, I'm not even sure if I could walk round that high up."

"We'll just walk through here then and not bother with the wall walk."

They all got their phones out to take photos of the castle from the grounds. It was both beautiful and impressive – and old! Dan read from his phone "Lincoln Castle was built by William the Conqueror in 1068."

"Ooh, even older than you, Dad!"

"Ha bloody ha!"

They walked on the path, admiring the grounds until Freddie asked "What that statue? It looks royal."

They headed towards it, Freddie reaching it first and getting his phone ready to take a photo. "Oh, it's King George III. Jem, come and stand near it and I'll take a photo of you with it. Something to show your mum and aunt later."

They all posed for a few photos, then moved out of the way to let some Japanese tourists have a turn. It was a popular spot for Americans too, as they could hear several different U.S. accents as they walked round. It was August though, the peak of the tourist season.

As they came out of the castle, Lincoln Cathedral was straight in front of them.

"Wow! Look at that!" exclaimed Freddie, his phone swiftly pointing at the spectacle. It seemed to be almost sparkling in the sunshine.

"Gorgeous!" agreed Jemima, taking her own photos.

They walked through the arch to see the building in its full splendour. Dan took some pictures too. It was one of the most beautiful cathedrals he had ever seen. "It's famous for its Lincoln Imp, that's why the football team are known as the Imps."

"Aww, cute!" said Jemima, posing for a selfie with the cathedral in the background.

They returned to the street near the Tourist Information Centre, between the castle and the cathedral. "Now, kids, according to Google maps, if we go up here and turn left, we'll be heading back to the car park. Or we can just walk to the museum. Either way, it's up here."

They followed him up a pretty cobbled street with all sorts of interesting little shops. "Oh look! A book shop!" Indeed, it was. The pale green frontage showed it was in fact Lindum Books, so the three of them went in. They all loved bookshops especially independent ones.

"Lincoln used to be called Lindum Colonia, you know. That'll be how the bookshop got its name."

"Absolutely right! Hi, I'm Tanya. Let me know if I can help you with anything," said the dark-haired woman at the till.

"Thanks, we'll just have a browse round."

"Shame Mum's not here. You know what she's like with books!"

"Perhaps we can buy her something. Have a nosey round, see what she'd fancy."

"Oh Dad, look! There's a shelf for local authors over here." The three of them turned to look. "A lot of local history stuff, but there's a novel too." Freddie picked it up and looked at the blue cover. "*Welcome to Whitlock Close*" he read out the title.

"That's the last copy of those, they've been selling pretty well," said Tanya. "She's a local author and has signed the books too." Freddie opened the book to the title page and found the autograph. "Do you think your mum would like this, Jem?"

"Hmm. Not sure. It's hard to tell with new authors she's not read before. A-ha!" She reached over and plucked a book from a display table near the window. "Now I know she'd like this!"

"Ah, the new Elly Griffiths. Yes, that's a great read," commented Tanya.

"Yes, Mum's read all the Ruth Galloway series. Elly's always a safe bet and I know Mum hasn't got this one."

"Great, we'll have that then, please."

They continued to walk up the street admiring the brightly coloured materials in the window display of the fabric shop and the cute cuddly toys in another window. There seemed to be lots of arty-crafty shops. "You know Aunt Lizzie would love it here, wouldn't she?"

"Well, we can always come back if they're interested. It's only the 14th today. We've got another two and a half weeks or so."

"We turn left at that Greggs. That should take us in the right direction."

It was a pleasant walk; the day was fine and warm, and they took their time looking at everything. It was the first time any of them had been to Lincoln.

121

"What's that big building on the right?"

"According to Google Maps, it's a water tower."

"Oh, look at that school. How lovely going to school right opposite the castle!"

They passed the school on their right, Dan checking his bearings with Google Maps. "So, the car's parked over there" – he pointed to the left – and the museum is round here on Burton Road."

They went past the corner shop then along the street to a crossing. "Ah, it's over there!" pointed Dan. "We've just got to cross the road."

"It looks quite castle-like itself, Dad."

"It does. Very nice." He checked the time. "Oh, we're okay, we've got a good couple of hours before it shuts. Plenty of time to look round."

Becki

Becki and Lizzie had spent the whole day inside the caravan, though they'd opened the windows for some fresh air, as it was a beautiful day out there. Trudi had been a bit disappointed to only nip out for toilet needs in front of their caravan, but Becki was hoping Dan and the kids might volunteer to take her for a longer walk when they got back. Neither Becki nor Lizzie could summon up the energy, they'd had an emotional few days.

Becki was trying to find out why her sister was so down. She'd realised it had to be more than her mother-in-law dying. She didn't think Lizzie had met any of Ebele's family. She'd certainly never been over to Nigeria. So, she wouldn't be heartbroken about the old lady's death, there must be something else upsetting her, but so far, Lizzie had clammed up when Becki had asked her a few probing questions.

Shutting the door after another of Trudi's wees, Becki put the kettle on. "Herbal tea, Lizzie?"

As she walked into the lounge, she saw her little sister scrolling through photos on her phone while sobbing, tears running freely down her cheeks.

"Oh Lizzie, love, what is it?"

Lizzie shrugged and showed her the phone. A gorgeous picture of Lizzie and Ebele, all dressed up, out somewhere together, big smiles and arms round each other's shoulders.

"We were so happy, Becki. Look at us. She's the love of my life!"

"I know that, Lizzie, but why can't she still be? Have you broken up?"

"To be honest, I don't know. Maybe her going back to Nigeria has made her realise what she was missing. Maybe's she's homesick and wants to stay there now with the rest of her family. Perhaps she won't come back to England. To me. How will I cope without her?"

"What did she say in that phone call that upset you so much?"

"It's not what she said, it's what she didn't say that's upset me."

"Oh?"

"She didn't tell me she loved me."

"Ah."

"We always do, at the end of every call. But not yesterday. She put the phone down before I could even say it to her." The sobs intensified and Becki passed her a tissue to wipe her face with.

"Was she on her own?"

"No, Becks, it sounded like the house was crammed full of people. You could hear the voices in the background. They've got a huge family and I think everyone was there. Even her sister in America flew over."

"So, the house was full, and Ebele had loads of family around her. Maybe she didn't feel comfortable saying that kind of thing in front of an audience? Do her family know she's gay?"

Lizzie considered the question. "Her mum does, oh did – got to get used to using the past tense now, bless her - and I think her sisters. I don't know about everyone else. We don't really talk about it. What her family think isn't really relevant to our life together in London."

"No and rightly so. But it might be relevant to her life in Nigeria. What are things like over there? With LGBTQ plus stuff, I mean. Are they okay about it?"

"Homosexuality is illegal in Nigeria, although they don't think lesbians exist. There're no such thing as gay rights over there. It's Christian and Muslim predominantly, so they're really conservative politically. It's one of the things she loves about London – that we can walk round holding hands and we aren't going to be arrested for it. I mean, we sometimes get some stupid bolshy teens trying a wisecrack comment, but nothing worse."

"There you are then, that might explain a few things. Did she answer the phone?"

"No, it was a man. I asked him if I could speak to her."

"That could be it then. The man who answered your call knew it was a woman, so she couldn't say 'I love you' to another woman, if he was still in earshot."

Lizzie sniffed loudly and squashed her tissue in her fist before throwing it into the waste bin in the corner. She had stopped crying.

"I suppose you could be right."

"Hopefully I am. Then it'll just be down to that. Not wanting a scene or an argument with homophobic family members. Especially as her mum's just died."

Lizzie nodded, calming down. Becki gave her another big squeeze. "Look, give it a couple of days and ring her again. See how things are then. But don't break your heart over those three words."

Dan

The Museum of Lincolnshire Life turned out to be free, which was an added bonus. They walked through the shop, Dan promising he'd buy them something on the way out. The lady behind the counter told them where to start and off they went outside into a large courtyard with an array of sturdy play equipment in the middle to amuse the little ones.

"Oh, look there's an Anderson shelter! We learnt about them at school during our World War II topic."

"Yes, we did too, Freddie. We had to make one out of corrugated cardboard." They ran over and took photos of each other standing next to it.

"This is the yellow door she told us to go through. Let's have a look round in here," suggested Dan.

Inside there was a long corridor with replica rooms on the right, featuring all sorts of old items. The first room included vintage toys and Jemima's attention was automatically drawn to the big dolls' house at the back of the room. "Oh, I love dolls' houses! I think it's because I never had one as a child. They're just so small, but perfect. I love all the little details like the tiny food and cutlery. If I ever have a daughter, they are definitely having a dolls' house, even if it's just me that plays with it."

After looking at everything there for a few minutes, they moved along to look at all the other rooms including a bedroom with a bright red and white striped bedcover and a flowery potty underneath the bed. Dan pointed it out. "That was so much better than going to the outside loo in the middle of the night! When I stayed at Nan and Grandad's house in the '70s, they had a potty under the bed for me to use."

"You're not that old, Dad."

"No, but my grandparents had outside loos. I think they only got their inside bathrooms in the early 1970s and were still using potties for the kids. I definitely remember peeking into the outside toilets, even though we didn't use them by then. Nan and Grandad's was at the end of the yard and when you opened the door, all these spiders would run away, disturbed by the light and the noise."

"Ugh," shivered Jemima. "So pleased we don't have to worry about that now. Mind you, those caravan portaloos leave a lot to be desired."

"I guess they're the modern day version of potties really," observed Dan.

They moved on slowly past other rooms, taking their time to look at all the old treasures from years gone by, each one finding something of interest to comment about. "Mum would like this too," said Jemima, taking some photos with her phone. "She's interested in history."

"Me too," said Dan. "This is just my kind of place. Oh, you see that old sewing machine. My Gran had one just like it. She did a lot of sewing, made most of my clothes when I was little. Every time you'd go round, she'd want you to try something on. The floor was littered with pins. We always kept our shoes on when we went round there!" He laughed fondly.

There was a whole room devoted to the tools and devices of washing day. Dan reminisced about the mangle his grandma had, how it was used to squeeze the water out of the wet clothes before she'd hang them up to dry, folded over the line of rope strung across the back yard. "And now, we've all got washing machines and tumble dryers!" laughed Freddie.

"Things have certainly moved on in the last few decades."

"They really have, kids. Housework has become much less time-consuming. My gran used to have a laundry day once or twice a week because it would take that long to get everything done and you had to wait for a good drying day too. Or else the clothes were hung over airers in front of the fire. And now it takes, what, two or three hours to get your washing washed and dried?!"

"I'm pleased I wasn't a housewife in the 1960s and before. It sounds like so much hard work!"

"Oh, it was, pretty much manual labour. I think housewives were pretty fit and healthy back then. I know my grandmothers were never overweight or anything."

"Well, they didn't have a McDonald's in every town either!"

"Jem! You say that like that's a good thing! I beg to differ!"

"Good point, Freddie."

They walked through a display of military history fairly quickly, as it wasn't something any of them were particularly interested in – the Boer War and the American Civil War and all that stuff. But when it came to the display about the First World War, the kids paid more attention to the items in the museum, as they had learnt about it at school along with their topic on World War Two. They knew they had grandfathers who had been involved in World War Two, so it seemed more real to them, recent history from not so long ago.

After that, they emerged into a big room full of vintage vehicles from a terrifyingly high Penny Farthing bike to an eerie old hearse with a hopefully empty coffin inside. The kids spotted an old Butlin's bike and started chatting about holidays and day trips to the various holiday camps they had been to over the years. Dan had been to the Skegness one a couple of times as a child with his parents and he was telling them about the monorail and the giant white rabbit statue he had loved when he was little.

They all posed for more pictures in front of their favourite vintage cars and bikes, then gasped as they walked into the next room, which was even bigger, and the kids ran over towards the impressive tank there. "World War One Mark IV Tank" read Freddie from the poster on the wall. "Wow!" More photos were taken – and even uploaded onto social media, as they had a Wi-Fi signal again - and they all walked up and down looking at the trains, tractors and other vehicles. Dan took a picture of a little train or traction engine called Violet ("That was my Nanna's name!") and pointed out a little red Lincoln imp on the side of one of the smaller farm vehicles. "Ah, look at him, he gets everywhere!"

Once they'd looked round the whole place, they went back outside again and took more photos of the vintage Gentlemen's Urinal, which was really rather ornate, especially considering what it had been used for back in the day.

It was still sunny and very warm outside and they were relieved to be going back inside to see the rest of the rooms recreated in vintage style. There was an old Post Office, where Jemima strained over the rope barrier to admire the old stationery and postcards to one side of the display. There was a shop with loads of old clothes and material that Jemima was cooing over, commenting how most of the old fashions would be sought after again nowadays, seen as retro and vintage.

Soon they had finished the tour and were back in the shop, where Dan let them both choose a small souvenir gift each and he bought a 1970s memorabilia pack for Becki.

They quicky popped into a café for a drink and a wee, then walked back to the car park. It had been a really lovely day, interesting and informative, but loads of fun and they'd all enjoyed it. But it was time to go back to Silver Sands Bay now. Dan just hoped Becki and Lizzie had been able to have the heart-to-heart they needed and that Lizzie would be in a much happier place by the time they arrived. He cared about her and hated seeing her upset.

Becki

Dan, Freddie and Jemima arrived back at the caravan just before six o'clock. Becki put a veggie casserole in the oven to warm up, while Lizzie started to prepare a salad for everyone.

"Now, don't you dare tell me you've all eaten on the way home!" teased Becki, giving Dan a kiss and the kids hugs. "Because we've been slaving over a hot stove all day,"

"Well, a lukewarm salad bowl, in my case," added Lizzie.

"Smells delicious, Becki, thank you both. And Lizzie, it's good to see you smiling again."

"Thanks Dan. We've had a good chat, Becki and me and I'm fairly sure the thing was Ebele was just a misunderstanding, but I'll ring her in a couple of days and will hopefully find out for sure."

"Oh, that's good to hear, I've been worried about you. I don't like to see you down, when you're normally the life and soul." Dan gave her a half-hug around where she was adding a dressing to the salad, being careful not to knock anything over.

"So where did you go, kids? What did you see?"

"We went to Lincoln, had something to eat first then we saw the castle, cathedral, then we went to a museum. It was really good. Oh Mum, we've got you a present."

"Two," reminded Dan. He handed over the 1970s memorabilia pack from the Museum of Lincolnshire Life and she took it into the lounge and sat down to open it and look at the contents. "Oh wow! Nostalgia fest! This is great! Thanks, Dan!"

"And we went into a lovely local bookshop and got you this!" Jemima handed her mum the book in a paper bag. Becki opened it and smiled. "Oh Elly Griffiths, I love her. Is this her new one?"

"Yes, the woman at the book shop said it was Elly's latest so I didn't think you'd have it yet."

"No, I haven't, that's perfect. Thanks everyone."

"I've got a load of photos to show you." Jemima sat next door to her mum and put the photo gallery up. As they scrolled through the pictures, Dan whispered to Becki "How's she doing?" pointing his thumb in the direction of the kitchen where Lizzie was still sorting out the food.

"Pretty good!" she whispered back. "Hopefully we're sorted, at least for now. I'll tell you later."

After seeing Jemima's photos, she then looked through all of Freddie's photos, which were very similar, but after the final one, Lizzie announced the food was ready, so they all sat down to eat and continue chatting. The kids were full of their day and spent the next half an hour describing everything they'd seen and done during their day out in Lincoln. By the end of it, both Becki and Lizzie felt like they'd been there with them.

Lizzie

It was three days since she had last rung Nigeria. She didn't bother to take the dog this time. If she had another upsetting phone call, she didn't want the extra burden of looking after Trudi. She didn't want the responsibility. Becki understood and said of course it was fine to go out alone. Dan and Freddie were due over at the caravan for tea soon, so she left Becki and Jemima busy doing a bit of tidying up.

There was actually someone in the phone box when she got there! A teenage girl who presumably was talking to her boyfriend by the snatches of conversation she could hear. She moved away slightly, peering in the windows of the amusement arcade, until all the flashing lights and bright colours made her eyes hurt. She saw the girl vacate the phone box and took a deep breath before walking in herself.

She put her coins into a high pile and unfolded the piece of paper with the number on. Her heart beating far too fast, she dialled and waited. There was a click as it was answered, a pause, then a familiar voice saying hello.

"Ebele!"

"Lizzie, hi, how are you?"

"I should be asking you that."

"Well, you know, we're keeping busy, trying not to let the grief overwhelm us too much. There are still a load of family to feed, but it's a bit less hectic than it was."

"Oh, that's good to hear. It's going to be hard, but it sounds like you're managing okay." She paused to take a deep breath. "You know when we talked the other day?"

"Yeah. Of course."

"Were you being guarded with what you said, because of your family members being around?"

"Oh that. Yes, of course. You know what the culture is like over here. A lot of old-fashioned bigoted views, I'm afraid. Even within my family. Especially with some of the older relatives who are extremely religious and set in their ways."

"Are you alone now?"

"No, two of my sisters are here, but they're fine. They know all about us."

"I was so scared, Ebele. I thought I'd lost you."

"Oh Lizzie, darling, please don't cry. I hate being so far away and not being there to hold you, to reassure you."

"You still love me then?"

"Of course! Always and forever, you know that. Please don't doubt me."

"I'm sorry. I'm sorry for being so silly, so emotional, jumping to conclusions. So sorry."

"Hey, stop apologising! It's just one of those things. It's kinda hard to express emotions across a telephone line sometimes. You know what I think about you."

"Well, I thought I did. It was just you not finishing the call with our usual three little words."

"I did say them in my head, darling. I hoped you'd hear them somehow. I'm sorry you didn't get the message."

There was a pause. "How long do you think it'll be before you come home?"

Lizzie was still dreading the idea that Ebele would somehow decide to stay in Nigeria now.

"Hmm, it's August 16th now. I'm just checking the calendar. Erm, two weeks today, okay?"

Lizzie signed heavily and happily. "That would be great. I'm staying with Becki and Jem at the caravan for now anyway, so I can fit in with your schedule, maybe go home on the 29th, that would work out. Get everything ready for you coming back and meet you at the airport."

"That would be wonderful, darling, just perfect."

They chatted for a few more minutes about the arrangements for Ebele's mum's funeral and things going on with her family, now they were all together. Lizzie talked about the fledgling relationship between Dan and Becki and how well Jemima and Freddie got on.

"Aww, sounds like a ready-made family there, Lizzie, how lovely!"

"It really is. I hope it works out for them. I'd love to see our Becki settled again. Maybe have to start looking for a fancy hat and wedding outfit."

"Ah, while we're on the subject of love and matrimony, I've been thinking while I've been out here and missing you so much. Shall we get married when I'm back?"

"Married?"

"Oh, did I say the wrong thing?"

"No, not at all, you said the most beautiful thing. Of course, Ebele. I would love to marry you."

"Excellent, we'll start organising the details when I get home later this month then. Looking at venues and finding our wedding dresses and all that jazz."

Lizzie was crying again, but for much better reasons than earlier. "Oh God, I'm going to have to go. I'm out of money for the phone box. It's expensive ringing Nigeria from England."

"I can imagine. Don't worry. Call another time and it won't be too long now until I'm back home with you, my darling fiancée. I love you."

"I love you too."

Becki

Dan and Freddie were sitting in the lounge drinking tea when the door opened and Lizzie came in. Becki saw the tears streaking her red cheeks and went over to hug her.

"Oh no! Are you okay? What happened? Did you talk to her?"

Lizzie waved her away, walking into the lounge and addressing everyone.

"Yes, I'm sorry, guys, I'm crying again. But it's all good this time. Thank you for all your patience during these last few days, but we have sorted everything out and I have some big news for you."

She paused and everyone waited expectantly until Becki broke the silence and moaned "Come on! I'm not waiting until Christmas. Get on with it!"

"And the upshot of our conversation is…," continued a gleeful Lizzie, with a mischievous glint in her eyes. "That it would appear that Ebele and I are engaged to be married!"

There were whoops and cheers, hugs all around and a few more tears as everyone absorbed the happy news.

"Oh that's wonderful, sis, I'm really chuffed for you."

"I'm so relieved! I went into that phone box thinking I'd come out of it single and heartbroken, that she'd dumped me and was going to stay in Nigeria with her family. Instead, we have the most wonderful of conversations, she says she loves me and I come out of there engaged and over the flipping moon!"

"That's fabulous, Lizzie," said Dan. "I'm so thrilled for you."

"Can I be your bridesmaid, Aunt Lizzie?"

"Oh, I should think so, love. A big pastel pink bridesmaid's dress with puffy sleeves, I can see you in that!"

"Hmm, maybe I'll come bridesmaid dress shopping with you both myself," suggested Jemima, giving her aunt another hug.

The celebrations continued throughout tea and into the evening, and even the kids were allowed a small glass of white wine to toast one half of the happy couple.

CHAPTER SIX

Becki

The club they'd been to, when they'd seen the talented female singer, seemed to be the only venue in the area which hosted events suitable for dating. It seemed to have a bit of an identity crisis not knowing if it was a club with a variety of acts advertised, or a good old local pub. But whichever it was, it seemed the best place for newly dating couples to go to.

It was Friday night and the local pub-cum-club was hosting a quiz night, which Dan and Becki fancied going to. Lizzie had kindly offered to babysit the kids again, promising them another impromptu art lesson, so everyone was happy. Lizzie was on the old Cloud Nine all the time at the moment, since the momentous phone call with Ebele on Wednesday. Becki didn't think she'd ever seen her little sister so happy and that made her happy too.

Becki dug out a dress she hadn't yet worn this holiday – a three-quarters length short-sleeved dress in a dark green. It was a bit posh for a day out on the beach, but she'd packed it in case she took Jemima out for a meal in a nice restaurant. Not that they'd done that yet. She put her blonde hair up into a messy bun with a matching green scrunchie and applied a light layer of make-up.

Dan turned up just before seven o'clock. He was wearing a new blue striped shirt with the sleeves rolled up, tight-fitting jeans and his new shoes from the market. They headed back to the pub, holding hands as they walked.

"I'm so pleased for your sister, she seems so joyous now, buoyant even!"

"Oh, she is. Her and Ebele are just so right for each other. It would have been so sad if things hadn't worked out for them."

"Freddie's very excited about doing more painting. I hope Lizzie is prepared for lots of puppy-like enthusiasm."

"She will be, Jem's been going on about it since we arranged to go out. You know, it's funny. When Jem and I were driving over here on that first day of the holiday, she seemed like such a moody so-and-so, I was kind of dreading spending the time away with her in some respects. I thought it was going to be a bit of a battle. You know, moaning about stuff, how bored she is without the internet, all that teenage angst stuff, even though she's only eleven. But it's not really been like that. I mean, the odd time… and definitely about the internet, but overall, not really."

They walked through the door and joined the queue at the bar. The quiz didn't start until half past, but it was already filling up.

"Maybe the seaside air is doing her good, Becki?"

"I think it's really helped having you and Freddie around, you know. He's her age and they get on well. I'm hoping she can talk to him about going to secondary school too. She hasn't said much to me, but I think she's nervous about it. We've been on some great days out together and she loved going to Lincoln with you both. She seems to have kind of grown up while we've been in Silver Sands Bay."

"Well, that's really good then and if I have the tiniest part to play in her being less moody, I'm thrilled. I think Freddie would have more demanding too without you lot here. He'd have been wanting to go out somewhere new every day, spending all my hard-earned dosh on magazines or something."

"Oh, that reminds me, Dan. I'm loving that Elly Griffiths book. I've read two-thirds of it already. I'm reading it in bed and staying up to the early hours, it's such a page-turner."

"Oh, I'm pleased it was the right choice. Freddie wanted to buy you this book by a local author but – "

He stopped as he got to the front of the queue and ordered their drinks from a young barmaid he hadn't seen before. Looking round, he realised there were more staff working this evening. They were obviously expecting quite a crowd.

They walked over to one of the few empty tables and sat down. The landlord of the pub was dishing out pieces of paper and various pens. As he got to their table, he said "Hello again. Pleased to see you back. Now if you write your team's name on the top, then when you've finished all your answers, we'll come and collect the sheets from you."

They thanked him and paid him their pound each for joining in. All the money went into the prize fund together and the winning team took the whole pot.

"Oh blimey, what team name shall we choose, Dan?"

"I've no idea. What about merging our names together?"

"Danbeck? Beckidan? No, those don't work. Where do you live again?"

"Wetherby."

"Oh yes, not far from us. Hmm, nope, can't think of anything from Wetherby or Harrogate."

"Argh, we need Freddie here. He's good at this kind of thing."

"Ah." Becki banged her hand on the table, making the drinks wobble slightly. "Trudi's Tail Wags. Because when she sees us both, her tail wags. I mean, it's not great, but it's a name!"

"Well, it's better than anything else we've come up with."

The landlord announced they'd be starting in five minutes and the quiz would be organised into five sections – a music round to begin with, then TV, cryptic clues, the news and general knowledge.

"I'll be useless at cryptic clues," whispered Becki. "My mind just doesn't work that way. Might be okay in the other rounds, depending on the questions."

Dan wrote the team name on top of their sheet in block capitals and they waited for the first question to be read out.

Lizzie

Lizzie had already covered the floor of the lounge in sheets of newspaper and some of the sofas, although Trudi had dislodged some of the pages when she jumped up on the side and snuggled down to watch the chaos. Now Freddie and Jemima had a large bit of space each, big pieces of art paper on the floor in front of them as they tried to recreate the landscape painting Lizzie had set in front of them.

"Now this is a painting I did at the sea in Margate a couple of years back. I didn't realise it was still in my sketch book, but here it is. I never did anything with it, because I felt it needed more work doing to it. Maybe more subtler colours or some texture added, I'm not quite sure. But you can tell it's a view of the sea drawn from the beach. What season do you think it was painted in?"

"Well, the skies look grey, so I wouldn't think it was summer," replied Freddie pensively.

"But it could have been evening and dark," suggested Jemima.

"Actually, you're both right. It was autumn and about four or five o'clock, I think, so getting dark, but not pitch black. I wanted it to look a bit dark and eerie, slightly foreboding. I didn't want a happy, bright sunshine summer's day painting, I wanted it to look bleak. The seaside when the tourists go home. All empty and lonely."

They nodded. "Can we paint on the beach this week sometime?"

"Oh, I should think so. We'll pick a day depending on the weather. I'm sure your parents won't struggle to find something to do, while we're busy." Jemima guffawed. "I didn't mean that, Jem. Take those dirty thoughts away right now."

"Aunt Lizzie! I didn't mean – "

"Well, never mind, back on topic now please. So, I want you both to recreate this kind of scene. The beach, early evening in autumn, or winter if you'd prefer. The opposite of a romantic, picture postcard scene of a beach in summer. Paint loneliness, bleakness, it's a time when the beach is forgotten, unloved. See how much of that you can convey with your colours and your textures. I've got more large paper if you mess up so don't be afraid to experiment."

Trudi jumped down off the sofa and walked across both pieces of paper as she went to the door to be let out. "Trudi!" moaned Jemima. "You better not do that when you come back. You'll get paw prints all over my artwork."

The dog obviously took notice of the tone, if not the actual words. After tinkling on the grass outside, she came back up the steps and jumped straight onto the double bed where she had a little sigh and settled down to sleep.

Dan

The quiz had been a right laugh and they'd been very surprised, but happy, that Trudi's Tail Wags had finished third overall. The fact that the music round had been about 1980s hits was a big help to them, but they'd done pretty well in all five rounds, though admittedly Dan had covered the cryptic clues, not Becki, but she'd got full marks in the news section. As Becki had said to Dan, it was proof their old grey matter was still working, even if they weren't in their twenties or thirties anymore.

It was only half past nine, but instead of staying in the pub drinking, Dan had suggested they take a walk along the sea front, or the promenade as he called it, harking back to decades before. Becki always pictured women in corsets with teeny-tiny waists, wearing floor-length dresses and holding parasols when she heard the word promenade.

It was still a warm evening and would be pleasant taking a stroll before going back. Besides, he had things he wanted to say to Becki. She had readily agreed and they'd walked along holding hands, lost in their own thoughts, happy together in this easy partnership. Again, Dan was struck by how different it was to be in Becki's company compared with his ex-wife Melanie's. Freddie was right, they were totally different women. He was ready to take a chance.

They came to an old bench facing the sea. "Let's sit down here a few minutes, Becki."

"Your old legs aching?"

"Something like that. Look. I wanted to say something."

She sat down next to him, their knees facing inwards, towards each other. She looked so beautiful. He leaned towards her and soon they were kissing, longing and attraction mixed up with pleasure, caring and a small bit of alcohol.

She giggled at him. "Was that what you wanted to say? Because I didn't hear many words."

"No. Sorry. It was – well, I got carried away. You look gorgeous tonight. You're irresistible."

"Blimey, you'll make a girl blush!"

"But I do have something to say. Look, I know it's only been a few weeks – "

"Four weeks on Sunday."

"Ha ha, okay, you've been counting, nearly four weeks. Not very long in the grand scheme of things. But I feel we've made a connection, that we could really have something special here, something worth continuing after the holiday is over and we go back to our daily slog."

"I agree."

"You do?"

"I do."

"Oh great, that was much easier than I was expecting."

"I thought that kiss would have given you a clue. I mean, did I kiss you back or run for the hills screaming?"

"Yeah, good point, we definitely kissed each other, it didn't feel like it was just one way. So, this isn't going to just be a holiday romance then?"

"Well, that's not what I want. I'd love us to keep seeing each other. I mean, Wetherby and Harrogate aren't far away. We both drive. I'm sure we can fit each other into our busy schedules somehow."

"I certainly think we can."

"The kids will be pleased too. I mean, that's important, isn't it? We want them to approve, not hate the idea."

"It is important, but I'm sure we'll be fine. We all seem to get along really well. Like a family."

"Yes, like a family."

They kissed again, before Becki started to shiver slightly as the warm air started to chill. Dan put his arm round her, warming her up as she snuggled into his body. They slowly walked back towards Tall Trees Caravan Park and Becki's home for the summer, where some of their most loved people (and dog) were waiting for them.

Becki

They entered a caravan of absolute chaos! The noise of excited squealing and a tiny barking dog greeted them as they opened the door, but they didn't dare attempt to go into the lounge, as the floor was filled with all kinds of brightly coloured paintings and art tools littered all over the room.

Becki laughed at the shock on their faces as they registered the new arrivals. "Shall we go out and come back in again?"

"Sorry, Becki, we weren't expecting you back just yet. The dog could do with a quick walk, if you fancy it. Give us a few minutes to tidy up."

"No problem." Becki grabbed a light jacket and put Trudi's lead on, then they went back out into the night.

"That was a welcome!" laughed Dan, taking the lead while Becki shrugged her jacket on.

"I don't mind a bit of mess anyway, but we'll let them get everything put away, I don't want Trudi here walking all over their pieces of art."

"Besides," said Dan, pulling her towards him. "It gives us a chance to do this again."

They drew together for another long, loving kiss, until Trudi saw something move in her peripheral vision and tugged the lead in Dan's hand. "Oops! I think she wants to investigate something."

They followed her lead (literally) as she sniffed intently at the edge of the site where the grass met the trees and there was a patch of wild flowers. She stopped suddenly and started whimpering. Dan got his phone out of his pocket and turned the torch on, illuminating where the dog was sniffing. The first thing he saw was that the flowers were a bright purple colour in the torch light. Then he saw something moving.

"Hang on, there's something in there," he said. Becki took the lead from him and pulled Trudi back out of the way, so Dan could investigate further. Angling the torch this way and that to get a better view, he gently reached a hand out and hesitantly stroked something. "It's alive," he said quietly. "And it's warm."

"What is it? A rabbit or something?"

"No. Not quite."

He put the phone back in his pocket and reached back into the grass, lifting out something dark. "We need to go back to my caravan, where it's quiet."

They headed back there, turning the lights on as they went inside. Becki held Trudi at a distance as Dan put the tiny thing down onto his lap, holding it softly so as not to scare it.

"Oh my God!" exclaimed Becki. "It's a kitten."

It was tiny, almost all black which is why it hadn't been easy to see. But when Dan picked it up to check if it was bleeding anywhere or had any obvious injuries, he saw it had a beautiful white tummy. He also saw some tiny little nipples. "It's a girl. Looks okay, can't see any cuts or anything sinister."

Suddenly the tiny ball of black and white fluff let out a pitiful miaow. "I'll get her a drink; she might be thirsty." Becki got a saucer from the kitchen cupboard and poured some water into it from the tap at the sink. She took it over and put it nearby. Dan lifted the kitten and moved it, so her face was above the saucer. Soon the cat was lapping happily.

"Do you think she belongs to anyone?" Becki asked. "She looks a bit young to be fending for herself out there."

Dan shrugged. "I doubt anyone on the caravan site would bring a kitten with them. Maybe it's a stray? We can put up some posters tomorrow, I know Lizzie's got some paper and we can ask around in the shops. I can get her checked out at a vets too, there's bound to be one nearby, I'll ask the guy in the supermarket."

"She's gorgeous, isn't she?" The kitten had stopped drinking and Becki was very carefully stroking her furry black head.

"Oops!" Dan said, noticing a trickle of wee coming from near the kitten's tail. "Time to clean the sofa then."

"She might be hungry, we should take her back to my caravan and see if she'll eat some dog food."

"Oh yes, Trudi will be thrilled! Is she any good at sharing?"

"Let's go and find out!"

Becki and Trudi went inside first. The lounge was clear of its earlier mess. Lizzie had presumably put all her art things away back under Jemima's bed, but there were some beautiful paintings out on display on the little table and around the caravan windowsills.

"Wow! Haven't you two been brilliant?" Becki said to the kids, as she came in with Trudi. "These are all gorgeous! I'm so impressed. Have you enjoyed your art class?"

"Oh yes," began Jemima. "It was great fun; Aunt Lizzie says we should keep up the art and we could be really good." She stopped abruptly, noticing that Dan had walked in and seemed to be cradling something small and furry in his arms. "What is that?" she asked reverently.

"It's a kitten, Jem," replied Freddie sighing. "Can't you tell?"

"Well, yes, okay, I can see it's a kitten, smart arse, but why's it here? Presumably you didn't win it at the pub quiz?"

"No, we came third. Besides, I'm sure they aren't allowed to give away pets as prizes nowadays."

"I won a goldfish at the fair in 1978," piped up Dan.

"Things were different then. Anyway, Trudi sniffed out this kitten in the flowers at the edge of the site, in that grassy bit. She's had a drink of water at Dan's…"

"And a wee!"

"Yes, Dan, and a little wee and now she's come over here to see if she's interested in nicking any of Trudi's dog food."

"Can we keep her, Mum?"

"I've no idea yet, Jem. We don't know if she's a stray or feral or if she belongs to someone. Best not to get your hopes up, love."

Freddie looked up at the tiny kitten, being cuddled in his dad's arms, her eyes tightly shut and a little purr coming from her. "She doesn't look feral to me."

"Maybe she just appreciates a little bit of love and kindness?" suggested Dan. "Anyway, we need to go to bed soon, it's late now."

"No! Can't we just see how she gets on with Trudi's food first?"

"Yes, have a cuppa before you go," said Lizzie from the kitchen, as the kettle finished boiling.

"Okay, one cup of tea and a few minutes of kitty observation, then it's bedtime. I want to take her to the vets tomorrow and get her checked over, so I'd like us to be up relatively early in case we have to wait for an appointment."

Dan

Dan and Freddie were back from their morning visit to the neighbouring supermarket. They'd needed more bread, milk and cereal, so while they were there, they had questioned the staff about the kitten. Everyone thought it would be a feral kitten, as they said they had often spotted stray cats in the grass and near the trees. One of the women who worked on the till said "You'll often see a mum cat with a litter, then the next time you see her, she's maybe got one kitten left. Maybe in this case, the kitten survived but the mum didn't make it. It's very sad. We're right near that busy road, you see, it's not a place for cats and kittens to thrive here."

They all promised to ask around if anyone knew anything and the man who owned it wrote down the address of the vets he used for his dog, explaining it was in the village, just over a mile inland.

Dan dumped his shopping in their caravan, then they both headed over for Becki's. They knew she woke up early, but were surprised to see everyone awake, up and dressed when they were let inside.

"My, Jem, you're up early!" teased Dan.

"Yes, we've all been on kitten watch since about half seven," explained Becki as she came over to give Dan a kiss. "She's settled in really well, eating and drinking – "

"And peeing and shitting – "

"Yes, thanks Lizzie, just because you stepped in a little parcel this morning."

"Yes, I did. Little sod," moaned Lizzie, though not without an obvious smile creeping onto her mouth at one corner.

"So, she's been okay then?" asked Freddie.

"Yes, great!"

"What does Trudi think to her?"

"Well, as you can see, she's in a huff. She's still in bed and hasn't come out to see you. I think her little wet nose has been put out of joint."

"Oh, bless her, can I go and see her?"

"Of course you can, Freddie." He went off into the double bedroom and sat on top of the duvet stroking Trudi's little red body, as she slowly decided to respond to the attention and show him her tummy.

"I've been to the shop with Freddie just now and no-one knows of any kittens, they think she's probably feral and that maybe her mum got hit by a car or something, so she might well be an orphan."

"Awww, bless her!" Jemima let out a little sob but coughed it away.

"The man at the shop gave me the address of the local vets, so I thought I'd take her for a check-up and see what he thinks."

"Can I come?"

"Of course, Jem."

"Okay, well you take the kids then and I'll get Trudi walked," said Becki. "Then she might feel a little less pushed out by wonder kitty here!"

Becki

She only had to wait about twenty minutes after getting back from her dog walk and Dan and the kids drove up with the kitten and two big carrier bags filled with stuff.

"That was good," explained Dan. "They saw us pretty much straight away. The vet checked her over and she's fine. Slightly underweight but he gave us this kitten food which should help her put weight on. He is sure she's old enough to be away from her mum, but still needs special age-appropriate food. Luckily, he stocks it. He also treated her for worms and fleas, just in case. If we don't find her owner and decide to keep her, he said we need to think about getting her microchipped too."

They emptied out the big bags. As well as the special wet and dry food for slightly malnourished kittens, there was a collar, a cat carrier, two bowls, a litter tray, cat litter and a comfy-looking soft cat bed.

"That must have cost you a fortune!" said Becki.

"Ah, don't worry. It's all the stuff the kitten needed."

"But what happens if we find its owner? All this will go to waste."

"Nah, I'm sure we could find another cat somewhere that needs a home. I'd forgotten how nice it was to have a pet until I met your Trudi."

"That sounds like a plan then. Shall I go and ask around the arcades and chip shop and all the places up there, to see if they know anything about her? I've got some photos on my phone to show them, if need be."

"Great idea. I'll sit down and have a cuddle with – oh, has anyone thought of a name for the kitten yet?"

She was greeted by shaking heads and blank faces. "Well, we can all have a think then, I'll go and ask around the shops."

Dan

It was Sunday and Dan and Freddie had decided to go back to Skegness. Freddie wanted to get some funny postcards to send to a couple of his friends and he wanted to check his social media and share photos of their adopted kitten.

No-one in Silver Sands Bay seemed to know anything about the stray, so for the time being she was staying with Becki, Lizzie, Jemima and Trudi. They were all trying not to get too attached to her, just in case an owner did turn up to claim her, but Dan was quite sure she was a stray and therefore legitimately homeless. They hadn't been able to persuade any of the females to join them on their day trip. They all said they needed to be with the still unnamed kitten and wouldn't dream of leaving it.

It was quite a warm day, but the sun was hiding behind clouds, so they didn't have to worry about the oppressive midday heat they'd dealt with last time they'd been to Skegness, when Becki had been especially cautious about the sun hats and sunscreen. Dan parked in the same place as before and they walked down onto the beach, checking their phones and smiling at the little kids enjoying the donkey rides on the sand.

One donkey took a bit of a detour and headed over towards Freddie, who stroked it on its nose. Checking its noseband, he saw she was called Flora. "Hello Flora!" he said. The lad leading it turned the donkey back in the right direction with a grin. "She's always doing that, wandering off to see folk, she's right sociable!" The little boy on her back was laughing with glee at the extra excitement. "Bye Flora!" said Freddie.

"You've made a friend, Freddie!"

"It certainly looks that way. I was thinking – "

"Oh, not this early in the morning, son, you know it's bad for you."

"Cheeky sod! No, I was thinking about the kitten with no name. The donkey was called Flora."

"So, I gathered."

"Well, that would suit our kitten because she was found in that patch of flowers."

"Oh yes, I see. Flora. It's very nice. We'll talk to the girls later and see what they think."

They ignored the doughnut kiosk this time, instead choosing to have a proper meal. There weren't many options to eat anything healthy on the seafront, so they decided to stick to the tried and tested fish and chips again.

They were seated inside the shop, drinking hot cups of tea. They had just finished their chippy dinner when Adam rang. He was their next-door neighbour and had been keeping an eye on their house while they were away. Dan looked anxious as he answered the call. "Hi Adam, is everything okay?"

Becki

The kitten was absolutely adorable, they were all falling in love with her and even Trudi seemed to have resigned herself to not being the only pet anymore and had apparently accepted her. The dog and cat happily ate their meals side by side and if the kitten left anything, Trudi knew she was allowed to eat it, but only if the kitten had walked away. It was a good arrangement for the little dog.

"I hope we find a name for her soon, Mum. We can't keep calling her 'the kitten' forever."

"Maybe Dan and Freddie will think of something."

"It doesn't look likely she'll be claimed, does it?"

"Well, I guess it's getting less likely as the days go on."

"But will she go home with us at the end of the summer, or back with Dan and Freddie?"

"I don't know. I guess we'll discuss that nearer the time. We'll all be staying in touch though. You know they only live in Wetherby and we're going to keep seeing each other, Dan and I were discussing it the other night."

"That's really good, Mum. It'll be wonderful for you to be in a relationship again. You already seem happier than you were before the holiday."

"Do I? Oh, that's good. I really hope the relationship will work out."

"Oh, it will, Becki," added Lizzie. "You and Dan are so good together, it's obvious to all of us. You must remember you are allowed to fall in love with someone else. It doesn't negate anything you had in the past."

"I know. I just feel guilty sometimes. That I'm still here, alive and breathing, and Rob isn't."

"Don't feel guilty, Mum. It wasn't your fault. You did everything you could for him."

"You did, Becki. You know you did. Right, I'm off to ring Ebele again." Lizzie rattled a load of coins. "I'm pleased I'm seeing her in ten days. These telephone conversations to Nigeria are costing me a fortune."

CHAPTER SEVEN

<u>Dan</u>

"Dad, slow down, it's not safe driving this fast!"

"We need to get to the caravan, get our stuff and get home to Wetherby as soon as possible."

"What did Adam say exactly?"

"I told you. He said he's heard noises from our house, so had gone round to check things were okay and no-one had broken in. Melanie was there, bold as brass. When she saw Adam, she went into the garden to have a chat with him. Told him she'd moved back in."

"So, he thought you knew?"

"No, he was sure I didn't know, that's why he rang me. Luckily, we were here and had a phone signal. He's been a bit of a sounding board over the years, poor guy. He knows how things turned out with me and your mum, he knew about her jetting off with Edgar, leaving us both for a life of luxury. He knew I wouldn't just let her walk back in like nothing had happened."

"Why didn't you change the locks?"

"Freddie! It's not some American psycho thriller mini-series on Netflix. I thought we'd be, well, all British about that kind of thing. I thought she'd have got rid of her keys or rang me before deciding to turn up out of the blue."

"She did ring you, Dad. Remember that time we were in Skegness and she'd been ringing both of us, but we didn't bother returning her calls."

He looked thoughtful for a second, then nodded. "Oh yes, I do now you've reminded me. But that still doesn't give her the right to move back in. It's not her bloody house anymore!"

Dan turned the car into Tall Trees Caravan Park. "Right, five minutes to just grab your basics. You've got everything you need at the house really. Don't be long. The sooner we get back to Wetherby, the quicker we get this sorted and send your mother out on her ear."

"What if she's got nowhere to go?"

"Son, she's not our problem anymore. If Edgar's dumped her, he can give her some money to stay in a hotel. Or she can get a job like everyone else, pay her own way for once, rent a flat."

They parked the car up by the caravan and dashed in, throwing a few essentials together before coming back out again, locking the door behind them. "Hopefully we'll be back in a couple of days. Get this mess sorted then come back and enjoy the rest of our holiday."

As they got back into the car, Jemima was just walking past from the shower block, her wet hair wrapped up in a brightly coloured towel. Freddie wound down the window. "Oh, we've thought of a name for the kitten. Flora."

"Oh, yes, fab name, I'll tell Mum and Aunt Lizzie."

"Come on, Freddie, we've got to go."

"Where are you going, Freddie? I thought you'd been to Skegness."

"We have. We've got to go back home."

"To Wetherby?"

"Yes."

"Why?"

Dan started driving the car.

"Mum's come home!" shouted Freddie through the open window, as his dad pushed his foot down on the accelerator.

Jemima was left there standing alone, her hair dripping, her mind racing.

Becki

Jemima came back from the shower block looking confused. "What's up, Jem? You look like you've seen a ghost."

"Dan and Freddie have gone."

"Gone?"

"Yes, home to Wetherby."

"Wetherby? Why?"

"I just saw them in the car as they were driving off. Dan seemed in a real hurry. He drove off while Freddie was still talking to me."

"How strange! What did he say to you?"

"Freddie?"

"Yes."

"He said the kitten's called Flora."

"Oh yes, I like that, that's pretty. And?"

"That he was going back, because - well, his actual words were 'Mum's come home!' – whatever that means."

"It sounds quite clear to me, Jem. Nothing ambiguous about those words. His mum must have moved back in. I didn't even know Dan was still in touch with her, he never said they were. Maybe he's decided to give her a second chance."

"No, Becki," Lizzie came over and wrapped her in a big soft hug. "He wouldn't do that. It's you he loves; you can tell by how he is with you. There must be some other explanation."

"Like what? Mum's come home is fairly easy to understand. What else could it mean?"

"I don't know, sis, but give him a chance. I'm sure he'll sort things out then be back here as soon as he can to explain it all to you in person."

"Look, I'm going out, Lizzie. Can you feed Flora, Jem?" She attached Trudi's lead to her collar and stuffed a couple of poo sacks into her jeans pocket. "I'll take Trudi for a walk on the beach. Blow off a few cobwebs."

Dan

"Dad, please slow down. I know you're angry, but we want to get home in one piece, not have a crash on the way."

"I'm sorry, son," The speedometer decreased from seventy-five to sixty. "I just can't believe the cheek of that woman. She pisses off – sorry – leaves us five years ago, we hardly hear a word from her in all that time, then she waltzes back in like nothing's changed." He sighed loudly. "Adam was livid on my behalf too."

It wasn't long before they arrived back at their semi-detached house and parked up on the empty drive.

"No vehicles then, Dad. Maybe she's left already?"

"Let's bloody hope so."

Dan stormed out the car, slamming the door hard and opened the front door with his key. As he went inside, it didn't take him long to tell where his ex-wife was. She had the television on loudly and was laughing along to whatever she was watching, probably some reality TV shite. Dan remembered how irritating he found her laugh. He marched into the lounge, grabbed the remote from the coffee table and turned the TV off.

"What the fuck are you doing in my house, Melanie?"

"Well, that's not the welcome I was expecting. I've come back, honey. I thought you'd be pleased to see me."

"You've even got a bloody American accent."

"I know, isn't it cute? I think it makes me sound sophisticated."

"You couldn't sound sophisticated if you swallowed a hundred bottles of Chanel No. 5. I'll ask you again, what are you doing in my house?"

"But Dan, honey, it's our house, our home. We had so many happy years here together." She stood up and sashayed towards him, her best flirtatious smile plastered on to her over-tanned face as she reached up to put her arms round his neck and pucker up for a kiss.

"What the hell are you doing?" He threw her arms off him. "You do not have the right to come here without my permission and you certainly do not have the right to be mauling me like some deluded cougar. We are divorced!" His voice got louder as he spoke, and he

160

was aware he shouldn't be shouting in front of his son, but he could not believe this woman and thought shouting might be the only way to make her understand.

"But you can't forget us? We were the perfect couple, we were magical together."

"The only thing magical was the way you disappeared, Mel. You're my ex-wife. Ex. Former. In the past! Now just piss off out my house before I call the police."

Suddenly there were the old waterworks switched on again. Same old, same old. Just like a toddler. You said no to something they wanted, and the tears flowed.

Dan walked out of the room briskly and headed to the kitchen, followed immediately by his son. Dan reached up to the top cupboard for the whisky he kept for special occasions and poured a generous measure into a glass. He downed it in two gulps, breathing heavily as he tried to compose himself.

"It's okay, Dad. You're bound to be angry. She's in the wrong, she knows she is."

"I'm more than angry, son."

"I know. Look why don't you stay here for a few minutes and I'll talk to her, try to find out what's exactly happened, how come she's back here."

His father nodded. "I'll come with you, but I'll stay just outside the room. I'll try to shut up and let you two talk. If I try to ask any questions, I'll just end up yelling at her. But I need to know what's going on. Why she's turned up all of a sudden."

He poured out another whisky and followed his son. Freddie walked into the lounge and sat on a chair, away from his mother who was curled into the foetal position on the sofa. She reminded him of Flora the kitten, though not so cute and much more manipulative.

"What happened then, Mum?"

She looked up at him and wiped her tears away with beautifully manicured hands. "I decided to come back. I want to be with you and your dad again."

"No, Mum, I'm not interested in the bullshit." Dan cringed at his son swearing, but stayed silent, listening in the background. "Why are you here? What happened with Edgar?"

"Edgar was nobody, Freddie, you know that. No-one important. It's you and your dad I love, I've always loved you both."

"Except for when you bogged off five years ago, for a better life in the States with your rich sugar daddy lover."

"You go, son!" muttered Dan. His little boy was impressing him and to be fair, doing a much better job of talking to Melanie than he had managed. Freddie's voice was steely calm, his words measured, and he was holding himself upright on the chair, looking straight at his mother.

"That's all over now. I've seen sense and come home. Back to the two guys I love the most."

Dan rolled his eyes. She would never have made it in Hollywood, her acting was terrible.

Freddie wasn't buying it either, Dan was pleased to see. "So, what happened, Mum? Did Edgar dump you?"

The tears reappeared, a streak of black mascara following them down her face. "Don't be vulgar, Freddie. Our relationship did come to an end, yes."

"How? You mean he found someone else?"

His mother nodded slowly, her head down, wiping away another tear.

"So, you weren't needed anymore then?"

"Surplus to requirements," she replied quietly. "He replaced me. With someone thinner and younger."

"But why come back here? Why not stay in America with all your new mates?"

"I didn't really make friends there. It was always just me and Edgar. That's how he wanted it. I mean, sometimes we'd go to some posh do, and I'd be gracing his arm in my newest dress, but I didn't really know the people there. They were Edgar's friends, not mine. More like business associates, I guess. All they ever talked about was money and all the posh foreign destinations they'd been to."

"Oh yes, I saw your photos on Instagram. You've been everywhere!"

She nodded. "Yes, I went everywhere. For a while. But now I'm home."

Dan stepped into the room. He felt it was up to him to take over the conversation now. Freddie had done a great job, but he couldn't be expected to sort out all the practical arrangements of this dilemma they found themselves in.

"Freddie, make us a couple of coffees, can you?" He winked at his son, who half-smiled and walked off towards the kitchen.

"Look, Melanie, I'm sorry you're in a pickle. It's all of your own making though, you need to see that. We don't owe you anything. Did you really think you could walk out for five years, then just saunter in like nothing happened?"

"But you love me, Dan, you've always loved me."

"No, Melanie. I don't love you. Not anymore."

She looked up at him standing in front of her. He had to admit she looked distraught. "But you always did?"

"I did, yes, but not now. I stopped loving you not long after you walked out that door for your brand-new life. You left me, you left your son! We made a new start, a new life without you. We coped – in fact, we thrived. And we moved on. The two of us. Without you."

She stood up again, pouting, another attempt to woo him with her physical charms. Dan just thought she looked pathetic and held his arms up to keep her away. "Do not come near me!" She slumped back down in the chair of the sofa, as the leather let out a hiss of air at the sudden movement.

"You moved on, Melanie, you can't move back."

"But you haven't moved on, Dan. I can come back to you. Be your wife again."

Freddie re-entered the room, holding two coffees which he put down on the table between his parents. "Dad has moved on actually. He's got himself a lovely girlfriend and they're very happy together. We're all very happy. We don't need you."

He went back out of the room to fetch his own cup of tea. Melanie was following his body with her eyes, her mouth open in an unattractive way.

"He's right, Melanie. You're not part of my life anymore. You'll always be Freddie's mum and you'll need to do some work on that, if you want to have a proper relationship with him again. But there's no place for you here with me. That place belongs to someone else now."

"But where can I go? Where can I live?"

"Didn't Edgar give you any money?"

"A bit. But not enough to buy my own place."

Dan harumphed. "Oh no, poor little rich girl, eh? Well, you'll just have to get yourself a job."

"But what can I do? I don't have any qualifications, or any work experience."

"I'm sure you could get a job at a pub or working in a shop or cleaning."

Melanie was shocked, as though Dan had just got a gun out of his pocket and pointed it at her. "Cleaning?"

"Well, you did a bit of it when you were here. Admittedly not to a great standard, that's why we ended up getting someone else in to do it, but I'm sure it'd come back to you in time."

"But I still need somewhere to live."

"What about your friends here? You had loads when we were together."

"Most of them took your side. The others I lost touch with once I was in the States. I didn't think I'd need them in my new life."

"That's typical of you, I'm afraid, Mel. Pick people up when they're useful to you then drop them off a high cliff when you don't need them anymore. Absolutely and completely selfish."

Freddie sipped his tea and leaned against the wall near the fireplace. "Maybe we could let her kip on the sofa for a couple of nights until she finds a flat and a job, Dad?"

Dan thought about it for a couple of minutes, draining his cup of coffee, feeling it merge with the hot whisky taste in the back of his throat. "I guess so. We're not heartless enough to make her homeless after all."

Melanie shot up off the sofa, heading towards him once more. "Will you just sit down, woman!" he yelled. "How many times do I have to tell you? We're not together, we won't be together ever again. I don't love you, I love someone else."

Oh my God, he did love Becki, he did.

"You can sleep on the sofa. Two nights and that's it. Go out and buy the local paper tomorrow, get flat hunting and looking for jobs."

"Why can't I have the spare room at least? A decent bed?"

"It's an office now. There's no bed. Only a desk and an office chair and I don't think you'll find either of those very comfortable to sleep in. It's the sofa or nothing. I'll get you a duvet and a pillow."

He left the lounge followed by Freddie. "If Mum's here, we can't go back to the caravan yet, can we?"

"No, son. I'm not going back to Silver Sands Bay until this stupid mess is sorted and that bloody woman is out of our hair."

"But what are Becki and Jemima going to think?"

"I don't know, that's what I'm worried about. Maybe we could see if a text message would get through. What's Jem's number?"

"I've no idea. I didn't need to ask her. Haven't you got Becki's?"

"No, there was no point as the phone signal was so dodgy and our caravans were in waving distance of each other. I was going to get it off her at the end of the holidays. Oh shit! I wonder what she thinks of me. What was it you said to Jem? Exactly."

Freddie thought back. "Apart from telling her the cat's name, I just said 'Mum's come home.'"

"Mum's come home?"

"Yes."

"Oh, good God! She could take that several ways. Well let's hope we can sort out your mother's bloody mess as soon as possible, then get back to the caravan site and explain what the hell's been happening."

Becki

She knew she was withdrawing into herself, but it was what she always did and she didn't know how to stop it. She was staying in bed longer in the mornings, going through the motions of preparing meals, making stilted conversation with her daughter and her sister, taking the dog out for long walks by herself. She felt so shocked and disgusted and humiliated. How wrong she had been to take

Dan at his word and think he was being honest. All those things he had said to her, it was just sweet talk, nothing real or genuine. There she was giving her heart to some bloke she'd known five minutes, believing all his lies, only for him to go back to his ex-wife.

"I'm going out, I'll be back in an hour or two." She grabbed her coat and bag and left the caravan. It felt oppressive, claustrophobic. She knew she was imposing on Lizzie, expecting her to look after Jemima, but she had to get out in the fresh air before she couldn't breathe. She felt she was drowning. Like her daughter would have done if Dan hadn't been there.

She couldn't cope with all the thoughts, the memories, everything was tinged now, it all felt dirty. All those wonderful times they'd spent together were shadowed by a dark cloud full of rain. She knew how it ended now. It didn't end with love and maybe marriage – yes, she'd let herself daydream about that already. It didn't end with everyone living happily ever after. No, it finished here, now, like this. Him back in the arms of his ex-wife, her going to the pub by herself to drink and forget.

As she walked in, the landlord acknowledged her, and she raised a weak smile in return. He obviously knew better than to ask too much. She requested a large glass of gin and tonic and went to sit by herself in a corner, out of the way. That's where she wanted to be – alone, hiding, invisible, ignored.

Two more big glasses later, she could feel the edges of her vision blurring satisfyingly. Her thoughts were blurred too, and she sat there listening to the jukebox playing old songs, singing along quietly to herself. Suddenly she looked up to find three men asking if the other seats on the table were free. Of course, they were, but she didn't want them sitting there. She wanted to be on her own. She shrugged but they sat down anyway.

The men stunk of beer and cannabis. It wasn't pleasant. Looking up at them, she saw they were in their thirties, maybe early forties. They started leering at her drunkenly. "Hey, love, what's your name then?" "You here alone?" "Looking for some fun, darling? I'm sure you are!" Their voices assaulted her, merging into one endless question. She started to feel dizzy and put her head in her hands to try to stop it. They were laughing at her. She wanted to get out, but they were blocking her way.

"Right, lads! Stop that now!" The raised voice belonged to the kindly landlord. "Leave her alone!" Becki felt her arm being gently lifted up, the lads were shoved to one side, and she was moved out of their way and taken through the bar into a back room. She sat on the chair she was offered and began to sob.

The man reappeared with a big mug of sweet black coffee. "Here you are, you drink that." She did as she was told. He pulled up another chair and sat in front of her. "They're harmless really, but I could see you were feeling uncomfortable. Are you okay now?"

She nodded, continuing to drink. "It's all a bit too much at the moment. Sorry."

"That's okay. I see your man isn't in here with you tonight. Is that the problem?"

She nodded but couldn't speak.

"Okay, I understand. Well, I'm John, what's your name, love?"

"Becki," she stuttered.

"Right, you drink up, then I'm walking you home. I think you need a bit of company. Are you staying on the caravan park?"

"Yes. Tall Trees."

He reached up and pulled an old brown jacket off a coat hook she hadn't noticed. She put the empty mug down and stood up. "Thanks John. I'm so sorry for being such a pain."

"Ah, you're not a pain. Let's just get you back safely."

Lizzie

There was a knock at the door, which they weren't expecting as Becki had a key. Lizzie opened it cautiously. There was a man there, around sixty, holding tightly onto Becki's arm. "Hi, love, are you Becki's sister?"

Lizzie nodded.

"I'm John, the landlord of the pub. She's had a few gins and there were a few pushy blokes, so she was getting a bit upset. She's had some coffee and I thought I'd better bring her back myself. Don't worry, she's safe and sound."

"Oh, thanks John, we appreciate it."

"No bother. I'll be getting back then. Night all."

"Night."

Lizzie helped Becki in and ushered her through to the bedroom. She took her shoes and clothes off and tucked her into bed. She was fast asleep before she'd turned the light off. Lizzie went back into the lounge.

"Is Mum okay?"

"Yeah, she will be. Just drowning her sorrows in alcohol. Not a good idea really. It was kind of the landlord to walk her home."

"What do you think has happened? Do you think Dan's gone back to Melanie?"

"I don't think so for a minute, Jem. You saw how he was with your mother. You don't fake that amount of affection; he genuinely cares for her. No, I'm sure it's all just a big misunderstanding. I mean, look at what happened with me and Ebele. I was convinced she had finished with me. Ironically, it was your mum who told me it wouldn't be as bad as I thought it was. But when you're actually in the situation, it's hard to see out clearly. I trust Dan, I really do. But we'll just have to wait. I'm sure he'll come back and explain everything, just as soon as he can. In the meantime, your mum's probably going through every possible scenario in her head."

Not long afterwards, they both went to bed, Jemima in her single room, Lizzie squeezing into the double bed alongside her sister who seemed determined to take up as much space as possible. Even Trudi decided not to bother trying to find a place in the bed that night and, in the morning, Lizzie found her fast asleep in the kitten's bed, Flora snuggled up in the curve of Trudi's warm furry tummy.

Dan

Dan wasn't quite sure where he was finding the patience from to deal with Melanie, but he was just trying to focus on the end goal – get her out, then get back to Silver Sands Bay as soon as possible. Melanie was being very difficult. She obviously wanted just to move straight back in here and for things to go back to what they had been five years before, despite him explaining to her countless times that it wasn't an option.

She was being incredibly lazy about everything. She expected Dan and Freddie to run round after her – to run her a bath, fetch her food and water, wash her clothes. Freddie did so at first, feeling a bit sorry for her, but he soon got fed up and began refusing to help her. "You're just going to have to learn to be self-sufficient, Mum. We're not going to run around after you anymore. You're perfectly capable."

Dan had been scouring the internet for flats and jobs, but Melanie had pooh-poohed everything he'd suggested. The flats were too small, didn't have a garden, were in a rough area, the list went on. "Look, how much did Edgar give you?"

"Only five hundred pounds. That's not enough to do anything with."

"Right, well there's a flat here to let, I'll ring up to get a viewing. It's about a twenty-minute walk away, right near to a load of shops, a pub, hairdressers, all sorts. There's a whole little retail centre going on there. You'd be bound to find something to do, some little job."

He could tell she was sulking; he'd seen it so many times before. This time, he was resistant, he wasn't going to give in to her demands. She was a grown woman, not a spoilt little eight-year-old. It was three days since he'd left Silver Sands Bay and he didn't plan to be away much longer.

He rang the agency and booked a viewing for that afternoon. If she didn't want to go, he'd see it without her. She didn't need a big luxurious place. There was only one of her. One bedroom, a kitchen, bathroom, lounge. That was all. He'd happily pay the rest of her deposit just to get rid of her. There was no way she was staying on his sofa for the foreseeable, he had his new life to get on with. He had absolutely no intentions of being dragged back to the past.

In the end, she did come with him, but barely raised her head to look at anything and her silence told him exactly what she thought of it. But it was perfect for her really. As well as being near a variety of shops – and therefore job opportunities – there was a doctors nearby and it was a five-minute walk to Tesco.

"It's perfect!" he said to the letting agent, Mr. McCoy, at the end of the visit. "She'll take it."

"Oh wonderful. Thank you, Mr. Armstrong. Do you want to sort out the paperwork now?"

"Sure. Why not?"

They walked into the kitchen together, while Melanie stayed where she was, staring out of the window.

A few minutes later, they came back in, and Dan tapped her shoulder. "Right, that's that all sorted then. Come on Mel, let's go to that café over the road, get some lunch and then have a look round."

The agent saw them out and shook hands with Dan on the doorstep. "I'll meet you here tomorrow at two o'clock then to hand over the keys and go through the final bits."

"Perfect, thanks."

Mr. McCoy headed for the smart Porsche parked across the road, while Dan steered a silent Melanie over to Tina's Tea Shop where he ordered them both an afternoon tea - scones with cream and jam and a big pot of coffee with cream. He hoped the sugar and caffeine would drag her out of the almost-comatose state she appeared to be in. Obviously becoming a grown up and looking after herself was going to be a shock for Melanie, who had gone straight from living with her doting parents to living with Dan, then Edgar. It was about time she understood what it was like to fend for yourself, not scrounge off others.

They ate and drank in virtual silence. In the end, Dan had worked himself into another quiet fury and spoke the first words. "Didn't you ever wonder how your son was getting on?"

She looked him in the eyes. "I sent him birthday and Christmas cards and presents."

"Yes, you did. But that's not the only thing a mother does, is it? It wasn't enough. It was barely bloody anything! Why didn't you ring him? Come and see him? Take him out somewhere?"

"He was five. We could hardly have a long conversation on the telephone."

"Yes, he was five. He's eleven now. He's got his own sodding phone. It was always an option. You just never tried. You're bloody lucky he's still talking to you at all."

She put her cup down and swallowed the last bit of scone. "I know. I'm sorry."

"It's not me you need to apologise to. It's our son. Your son. He thought you'd forgotten him, you know. Five years old and he's walking round the house, wondering where his mother is. I lost count of how many nights he'd be crying, asking me what he'd done wrong, why you'd left him. It was heart-breaking."

The waitress came over to clear the table. "Can I have the bill, please?" Dan asked her. He paid for it all, then walked back outside, Melanie a few paces behind him. He waited outside the café for her to catch up.

"I'll try to do better," she said meekly. "I want to be a good mother, I really do."

"Well, you need to talk to Freddie about that, not me." He indicated all the things they could see around them. "Look, you've got plenty of facilities here. You'll be fine. Shall we go into a few places now, see if they've got any jobs going?"

She shook her head. "I'm not strong enough right now. I'll look later."

"Well, make sure you do. I've bailed you out once here, but I'm not doing it again. I'll bring you here tomorrow, get you settled in then you're on your own. The flat's furnished, it's got pots, pans, cutlery, a kettle, toaster, microwave. You'll be fine. The electric and gas are paid until the end of the month, so you've got a good start there. Don't cock it up. The only one to get you out of this damn mess is you, no-one else. Oh, and you can give me your keys to my house too. I do not expect you ever to swan up and let yourself in like you did. Never! Do you understand?"

She nodded.

"Well, you better do."

Becki

The three of them were eating tea, a big cheese and potato pie Lizzie had cooked, the quintessential comfort food meal. Hale and hearty, as Becki and Lizzie's mother would say. Proper home cooking. Lizzie and Jemima were wolfing it down, Becki taking little nibbles every so often.

"I was thinking," she said, putting her knife and fork on the plate. "I think we should go home tomorrow."

"What? We've got nearly a week left of our holiday, Mum. Why go back so early?"

"It's not the same now, is it? I want to get back to Harrogate, forget about Tall Trees Caravan Park and Silver Sands Bay. Forget about stupid men who don't keep their promises and run back to their exes the minute they crawl out of the woodwork." Lizzie and Jemima exchanged a look but let her continue. "I've got some work to do before the autumn term starts anyway. It'll be good to get back."

"Well, I wasn't planning to leave until the 29th, sis, because Ebele's not back until the 30th."

"There's no reason you can't stay, Lizzie. I just feel I need to go home now. I've had enough of the seaside; the summer holiday is over for me."

"Mum! What about my summer holiday? This was our big chance to spend quality time together, remember, enjoy ourselves before I start secondary school."

"I know, Jem. But what is there we haven't done? What have you missed out on?" Jemima didn't reply. "Exactly. Look, I'm sorry, Jem. We'll sleep on it tonight and if you think of something you

176

want to do tomorrow, we'll do it then go home on Saturday. If not, we'll leave tomorrow morning. Lizzie can stay here as long as she wants." She smiled a bit then said "Right, I'm taking Trudi out. I'll see you soon."

She walked up to the seafront with the dog, the noises of the arcades and all the excitable kids on holiday fading into the background. She sat on the beach for a while watching Trudi run around off the lead, barking at the lapping waves and running backwards and forwards in the silver sand. Becki was trying to make her mind blank, concentrating on her senses like she'd heard people should do if they had panic attacks. She listened to the seagulls crying, felt the soft sand under her hands, smelled the salty sea in the breeze and saw the contrasting blues of the sky and the sea. She was thinking so much about the exercise that she jumped when she realised someone had sat down next to her.

It took a few seconds to recognise the woman out of context, her hair no longer tied back and under a hairnet, her face smiling lightly instead of frowning with concentration. But she still whiffed of fish and chips. It was Jean.

"Hello love. Becki, isn't it? Jemima's mum?" Becki nodded. "Haven't seen you for a while. I've still got some halloumi in for your girl, you know."

"Thanks Jean, but I think we're going home tomorrow."

"Oh, your daughter told me you were staying all summer."

"Yes, we were, originally."

177

Trudi came haring up the sand, long ears flying backwards and threw herself on top of Jean. "Hello, sweetie. Come and have a tummy rub with Auntie Jean then!"

Becki hadn't planned to tell Jean anything. She hardly knew her after all. But somehow, it came out easily And it turned out Jean was an excellent listener. It was a relief to tell her the whole story, culminating with how her and Dan had declared their intentions to have a proper relationship then the next thing she knows, he's tearing off in his car because his wife's come home.

"Love, I've seen you two together, I know how that man looks at you. He adores you. There's no way he'd go back to his wife, it's you he loves."

"Oh, but you can't say that for sure."

"I can. I'm sixty-five, I've been here a lot of years, lived a lot. I've been married twice, divorced twice. I know a rogue when I see one and your man is genuine. I've seen all sorts here over the years – holiday romances, flings, affairs, teenage love, break ups galore. I can spot a wrong 'un a mile off and your Dan isn't a bad one, you mark my word. There'll be some misunderstanding, some reason behind him running off like that. But I bet you anything, he'll be running back here as soon as he can, back to you. You just wait a bit longer, duck, give him a chance. You won't regret it."

She stood up, fussed the dog once more and shook the sand off her trousers. She started walking away but turned back towards Becki. "If I'm wrong, you can have fish, chips, halloumi and mushy peas all on me, deal?"

Becki stood up and ran over to her, giving Jean a big hug. "Deal. And thanks, Jean. You've been so kind."

"All part of the service, love. I'll see you soon. All of you."

Becki went down the beach to where the waves were coming in. Taking her shoes and socks off, she paddled at the edge feeling the icy cold water pierce through her mind. Was Jean right? Lizzie had said much the same thing. Could they see something she couldn't? Was Dan really different, was he genuine? She thought another couple of days here wouldn't be too bad. Maybe she should give him one last chance.

Trudi came running out of the sea, proudly carrying some seaweed in her mouth. "Wow, what have you caught there? Clever girl Trudi!" She rubbed her soft, wet head. "Let's get you home, shall we?"

Becki squeezed her wet socks then shoved them in her pocket but put her shoes back on at the edge of the beach. They headed back towards Tall Trees Caravan Park, Becki feeling much lighter and more positive, as Trudi proudly carried her bit of seaweed all the way back to the caravan.

Dan

Melanie had refused to pack up her stuff, so Dan and Freddie did it between them. She'd only been in the house less than a week, but her things had infiltrated every room and it took them hours to find it all. In the end, Dan said they had to stop and if they found more later on, he'd take it to the new flat another time.

They arrived there early. Freddie had come too, to see where his mum was going to be living. He told his dad he hoped she would want to have more of a relationship with him now she was back in

179

the area, but Dan warned him not to get his hopes up, she'd let him down big time before.

Mr. McCoy the letting agent was back in his impressive Porsche but didn't stay long. A few signatures on documents, the keys handed over and he squealed away in his big car.

The three of them went into the flat, Freddie going into every room and finding something nice to say about it, even as his mother followed behind with a sulky expression on her over-made-up face. "This is cool! Look, there's even a little garden at the back. You can sit out there with a book and a glass of wine and enjoy the sun."

"I don't read books," moaned his mother.

This immediately reminded Dan of Becki's love of reading. He absent-mindedly wondered if she'd finished reading that Elly Griffiths book he'd bought her. Or maybe she'd ripped it up in anger at him disappearing like that. But no, he didn't think she was the sort to rip up books, regardless of how angry she was at him.

Freddie seemed to be losing his patience with his mother. "Well, I don't know. Sit in the sun scrolling through Twitter or Instagram. Find some more pretty pictures to post."

"It won't be the same," she wailed. "Those gorgeous photos of me in Barbados, Canada, Corfu, Monte bloody Carlo for God's sakes, followed by what – the garden of a tiny downmarket flat in pissing Yorkshire."

"Well, yes, why not? Mum, this is real life, not what you have been putting up on Insta for the past five years. Take photos of your garden, your new flat. Buy some flowers, take photos of them. I mean, God forbid, you could even take a photo of me, your son!

Have you forgotten that?" He was crying now, snotty tears he couldn't stop running down his face. "Normal parents take photos of their kids, put them up on the walls of their living rooms. Kids they're proud of, you know? Look at this photo, my son made the school football team! You don't even know, or care, if I play football. You don't know my best mate's name, my favourite band, the TV programmes I watch, my best subject at school. You don't even know I was in hospital last year with a really bad infection?"

"You were in hospital?"

"We did try to ring you, Mel. We couldn't get through. I think you were in the Caribbean at the time."

"You weren't there for any of it, Mum, nothing. You lost all those years. Five years. And if it hadn't been for bloody Edgar dumping you, you'd still be out there with him on some bloody yacht in Jamaica sipping cocktails and eating fresh mangoes."

He went out the room and they soon heard the front door slamming behind him.

"I'm going now, Melanie," said Dan. "You've got everything you need, I think." He threw a twenty pound note out of his wallet and it landed on the floor near her feet. "That'll get you some food and drink. I'm going to see how our son is, now you've broken his heart for the second time. See you around."

Becki

When she got back to the caravan, she saw two anxious faces as she walked inside with the dog. Jemima held out a piece of paper. "I've come up with some things we could do tomorrow that we haven't done yet." She began to read the list. "We could visit

Mablethorpe, Cleethorpes, Chapel St Leonards, Butlin's, the seal place at Skegness – "

Becki stopped her in mid-flow. "It's okay. We're not going anywhere tomorrow."

"We're not?"

"No. Let's give it a couple more days and see."

"Oh great! Thanks Mum."

Trudi came over, sniffed Flora and dropped her piece of seaweed at the kitten's feet. "Miaow!" said Flora.

"Oh look, isn't that the sweetest thing!" exclaimed Lizzie. "Trudi's brought her a present."

The next morning, Jemima said "I'd rather like to go to Super Water World again, you know Mum."

"I bet you would, but I'm not planning on taking out a second mortgage, thank you very much!"

"Can we go into Skeg then to the seal place? I mean, they haven't just got seals there. They've got meerkats, penguins, alpacas. I saw a leaflet about it last time we were in Skegness. It looks great."

"Well, we could do but it'd mean leaving your aunt again with the dog and kitten to look after."

"I don't mind," Lizzie came out of the bedroom, in the middle of plaiting her hair. "I could do with getting some painting done, assuming these little furry rascals give me some peace and quiet."

"Well, if you're sure you don't mind? I could take Trudi out for a quick walk first, if you want?"

"Okay, you do that while I finish my hair, then you two get off to see these seals. Oh and take some photos of the alpacas for me, I love them, they're so cute."

"Will do."

An hour later, Becki and Jemima had parked up and were queueing to get into Natureland. It was another sunhat and sun cream kind of day and they were both suitably attired. Jemima looked up at the bright blue sky and said, "I think it's going to be a good day today."

"I certainly hope so. We deserve one of those."

CHAPTER EIGHT

Dan

They had hoped to leave Wetherby at eight or nine o'clock to get to Tall Trees Caravan Park by eleven or midday, but things hadn't gone to plan. Melanie had rang first thing, complaining something had fused and she couldn't get her electric back on. She'd also ran out of milk and had no money left. God know what she'd spent the twenty quid on already, Dan thought.

They packed up the car to go back to the caravan and Dan popped round to explain to Adam what had been happening, saying they'd be home again on the 31st and not to expect Melanie to move back in at all.

Driving back to the flat, Freddie was already talking excitedly about seeing everyone again in Silver Sands Bay, wondering how Flora was settling in and suggesting things they could do to fill the last few days of the summer holiday.

It turned out it was the iron Melanie had found in a cupboard that had shorted the electrics. Dan got them back on with one click and showed Melanie what to do if it ever happened again, though he suspected her first port of call would always be to ring him. He gave her another twenty-pound note and explained they were going away and that would have to last her.

"Any luck on the job front yet?"

"No," she answered.

"Have you even tried? Have you asked in any of the shops or anything?" She shrugged sulkily. She was so irritating. Dan couldn't understand how he'd managed to stay in a relationship with her for so many years. Perhaps he'd just ignored her many bad points in favour of her fewer good ones? "Well, you'd better get something sorted because that's the last bit of money you're getting from me. Get a job or apply for benefits."

"Benefits?"

"Well, yes. That's what people do. Go on benefits until they find employment. Do you have any better ideas?"

He didn't wait for a response. Freddie gave his mother a half-hearted hug and let her kiss the top of his head, then ran down the steps and got into the front passenger seat. Dan just started the car and drove off. He didn't give his ex-wife another glance. She wasn't worth it.

It was mid-afternoon by the time they arrived in Silver Sands Bay. They pretty much threw their bags into their caravan, parked the car where they were supposed to and jogged round to Becki's caravan, racing to see who could knock on the door first.

Lizzie opened it, a big grin on her face as she realised who it was. They were soon enveloped in her big loving hugs as she invited them in, automatically putting the kettle on. Dan and Freddie went into the lounge, Trudi rushing over towards them, Flora staying in the background.

"I'm sure that kitten's grown in the last few days," observed Freddie.

"She probably has, she's been eating really well. Poor Trudi doesn't get many leftovers now."

"Aww, bless her. Are the animals getting on okay?"

"Oh yes! They're even sharing a bed most nights!"

Dan picked up Flora for a cuddle. "Hello, baby cat and how are you doing?" She batted his nose with her black furry paw then licked it with her spiky tongue.

Lizzie made the drinks and brought them through with a plate of Custard Cream biscuits, which Trudi eyed up straight away, sitting underneath the table in case of any crumbs.

"So have you driven over from Wetherby today then?"

"Yes. We had a bit of a crisis and had to go home in a rush. Then we realised we didn't have any of your phone numbers, so we couldn't ring or text or anything."

"Not that we had any signal here anyway."

"Very true. Anyway, how is Becki? Was she upset?" His brow was furrowed as he looked closely at Lizzie for any reaction. This was what he was most worried about.

"Hmm. You could say that. John the pub landlord had to escort her home the other night after she'd drowned her sorrows. She was all for going back to Harrogate today, until Jem and I persuaded her – oh and Jean from the chip shop."

Dan looked confused, but figured he would work it all out eventually. "So where are they now?"

"Skegness. Natureland."

"Oh okay. I guess they'll be back soon then."

"Who knows?" Lizzie shrugged. "I think when they do get back, I should take Freddie and Jemima out somewhere. Give you two a chance to talk in private. I think there are some things you need to explain."

Becki

The two of them had really enjoyed themselves, it had been such a fun day, but they were both feeling tired now. It had been quite draining walking round in the heat despite their hats and regular reapplication of Factor 50 sun cream. They were looking forward to getting back to the caravan for a rest. Becki was hoping Lizzie would offer to cook tea, as she really didn't feel she had the energy to do it. If not, she'd nip to the little supermarket next door and buy a couple of veggie pizzas to stick in the oven. Maybe garlic bread too. And dough balls. She seemed to have got her appetite back.

They parked up then walked across to the caravan. The door opened as they approached and Freddie came out to greet them. "Surprise!" he said. Jemima gave him a hug and they went back in, Becki following. Dan was stood up waiting for her, but she avoided his eyes, walked right round him and sat down on one of the sofas, without saying a word to anyone.

Lizzie chivvied everyone round. "Right, we're taking Trudi out."

"I'm tired, Aunt Lizzie, we've been walking all day."

"Well, another hour won't kill you. Come on."

The three of them and Trudi left the caravan, shutting the door behind them and walked off in the direction of the main street.

The caravan was quiet for a few minutes. Becki was angry, Dan didn't seem to know what to say or do. If he'd been expecting her to rush into his open arms as though nothing had happened, he was going to be proved wrong.

"I need to explain," Dan finally began, picking up Flora again and stroking her soft back.

"You do, Dan."

"My ex-wife Melanie came back."

"Yes, Freddie told Jemima. Mum's come home, he said. Didn't happy families work out for you?" She crossed her legs to match the arms folded across her chest.

"It wasn't like that! Not at all. Look, shall I make us a drink then I'll go through it all?"

"If you like."

He made two coffees, took them through and started from the beginning.

"I was in Skegness with Freddie that day when our neighbour Adam rang. He'd been minding our house while we were away. Anyway, Melanie had moved herself back in. Turned out her American husband had kicked her out for a younger model and she'd come back to ours, thinking she could just move back in as though nothing had happened."

"What the fuck?"

"My thoughts exactly. Yep, just like that. She was homeless apparently. Still had the house keys, so thought she'd move back in. She said she'd tried to ring us, but of course, we were away and had no signal."

"Hang on, back track a sec. She got finished by her husband, still had the keys to your house, so moved herself back in."

"That's the gist of it."

"Oh my God, what a sodding cheek!"

"Absolutely. So as soon as Adam told me, we got our stuff from here and I sped back home to try to sort things out. I figured the sooner I could get her chucked out, the quicker we'd be back here, laughing about it."

Becki gave him a look which suggested she hadn't been doing much laughing lately and certainly wasn't ready to do so yet. Dan realised his mistake, smiled shyly and continued the story. "I thought we'd only be away a day, but of course it wasn't that simple. Things are always complicated where Melanie is concerned, I should know that by now. 'Twas ever thus. Anyway, Edgar – her husband – had given her five hundred pounds, paid for her flight back to England and the taxi fare to Wetherby. She told us she had no friends left to stay with, no income or any way she could start again. So she thought going back to the house was her only option."

"Hence assuming she could just rewind the clock and go back to being your wife all over again."

"Yep, exactly that. Completely deluded."

"Cheeky mare!"

"She's always felt she was a real catch, something special, like the world owed her a favour. It's just what she's like. Anyway I explained that was not an option, she was no way in hell moving back in with us and that she could only stay a couple of days until we found her a flat to rent. But of course, she didn't really want that."

"No, she wanted to step back into your house. Your bed!"

"Well, yes, I believe that was her intention. Anyway, she was on the sofa and we eventually found her a flat about twenty minutes away. I thought, if she's serious about being a better mother to Freddie, she can walk twenty minutes to see him. But we'll see what happens there."

"So, you got her set up with a flat for five hundred quid? How did you manage that miracle?"

"No, I had to give her the rest. But it was worth it to get rid of her and she's right near a whole load of shops and places she could find work, if she can be bothered to look. But I've told her she's not getting any more money from me. She's got to stand on her own two feet. I mean, she's forty-five. She's got to learn to cope on her own."

"So, you've set her up with a flat and given her money?" Dan nodded. "So does she think you'll be popping in for sexual favours every so often as well? Get a return on your investment?"

"Oh Becki, don't be like that. Of course, she doesn't. I made it very clear. I told her we were over as soon as she walked out that door five years ago. I told her I've moved on, I don't love her anymore and that I'm in love with someone else. She should have got the bloody message. I don't think I could have been any clearer than I was."

"You're in love with someone else?"

"Yes, of course I am."

She looked him straight in the eyes and asked, coquettishly, "Is it anyone I know?"

"Oh blimey! What are you like?" He put Flora down on the floor and she went over to her bed and snuggled down. She seemed to know that was all the affection she'd be getting for a while.

"My darling!" He knelt down in front of her, held both her hands in his and looked into her bright blue eyes. "This is me being completely honest with you. I do not love Melanie and haven't done for a long time. I love you. It may have taken this big stupid mess of a situation for me to realise it, but what I thought was an attraction was actually me falling head over heels in love with you. Yes, you! Becki Gibson. No-one else. And as I have realised this, it has also made me very aware that I don't want to be without you at all from now on. Not only do I want to keep seeing you after the holiday, but I'd also like us to look into moving in together."

"Wow! That's a lot to take in at once."

"I know and I'm sorry, but while I'm in full disclosure mode, I wanted to get everything out there. Cards on the table. Let you know exactly how I feel, so there won't be any more misinformation or miscommunication or whatever it was."

She bent forwards and their lips met. As they pulled apart, Dan looked at her again and said "And there's one more thing I need to say."

"What's that, Dan?"

"Can you help pull me up? My legs have gone dead!"

An hour or so later, there was a key in the door and three humans and a dog peeked round the side.

"Can we come in?" asked Lizzie. "Or will we be dodging gun fire and water cannons?"

"Nah, you're alright, sis, come in. We're fine."

"Aww, I can see that now," she said, as she saw Dan and Becki cuddled up together on the sofa. "Well, that's good to know. Oh, I walked past the chippy. Jean asked if you wanted all the works and who was paying? I wasn't sure what she meant, but I said I'd pass the message on."

"Ah yes, take my purse. Are you okay nipping back to get us tea from the chip shop?"

"Sure, no worries."

"Can you please tell Jean I'm paying for the whole meal and I'm completely, blissfully happy to do so." Lizzie gave her a puzzled look. "She'll understand."

Dan

That weekend was a three-day weekend, including the Bank Holiday Monday. They crammed as much as they could in to the hours available, knowing their holiday was soon coming to a close, but they managed to have a wonderful and fun-packed time. Lizzie looked after the pets while the four of them had another fabulous day at the overpriced, but still amazing, Super Water World. This time, they all had a go on the slightly harder twirly slides including one that was completely in darkness until they splashed into the water at the end. They all relaxed together in the jacuzzi and there were absolutely no tears from anyone this time – although Dan did comment his wallet was a bit emotional after he'd totted up how much they'd spent there. Even the alcohol-free cocktails they'd sipped in the jacuzzi cost twice as much as a pint at the pub in Silver Sands Bay!

On the Sunday, they had half a day out in Chapel St Leonards, which was a bit like a mini version of where they were staying – arcades, bingo, a café and the beach. It made a change though.

Then they went back to the market to get Becki some more books and they also nipped back to Skegness beach so Becki and Jemima could meet Flora the donkey, who the kitten had been named after.

On the Bank Holiday Monday morning, the weather was beautifully still, so Lizzie took Freddie and Jemima onto Silver Sands Bay beach and they painted the views for a couple of hours. They came back full of it and to be fair, their work was impressive. Lizzie was encouraging them to keep up their artwork and Dan promised to look into classes they had in the area, to see if anything would suit. He did try to persuade Lizzie to move her and Ebele closer to them, but sadly she couldn't be persuaded. They loved London too much to move, she insisted, though she promised they'd visit often.

In the evening, the pub had a drag act on called Big Bertha. Dan offered to babysit the kids and pets in Becki's caravan, while the two sisters went out together. He was feeling guilty about all the times Lizzie had stayed in, while the rest of them were out having fun. She was going back home on Tuesday and he wanted them to have some good quality sister bonding time. Plus, he thought he'd much prefer to play a few more board games with the kids and spend time cuddling the pets than watching a drag act.

Becki

"That was so lovely of Dan to babysit. We're going to have a great night out, just the two of us!"

"I hope so. The kids were so good this afternoon though, really dedicated, they worked so hard and I'm genuinely impressed with what they produced. Those seascapes were amazing. You need to make sure Jem keeps it up."

"I'll certainly try, Lizzie, I know if you say they have talent, that they really do. I value your opinion."

"And you know you'll always get it from me. Straight down the line."

They were met at the bar by John, a big smile on his round face. "Ladies! How lovely to see you both in here. And how are you, Becki? Everything sorted with that man of yours?"

"Oh yes! That reminds me, I owe you something." She leaned over the bar and gave him a kiss on the cheek. "That's to thank you for rescuing me the other night., I'm so grateful."

"Oh, it was nothing. I'm just sorry you needed rescuing in the first place. But I'm really pleased to hear things are fine again now. Gin and tonic, is it?"

"Yes please. Lizzie?"

"The same for me, thanks John."

He passed across two large gin and tonics, fixing lemon slices to each glass and adding a little parasol with a flourish and a grin. As Becki got out her purse, he waved it away. "On the house," he whispered. "But don't tell anyone!" He winked. "I can't give away free drinks to everyone. Just my favourite customers."

Lizzie pushed through the crowds with repeated 'excuse me's until they found a table for two. It was a bit too near the stage for their liking, but there wasn't much seating left. Twenty minutes until the cabaret started and the place was already heaving.

"These drag act nights are much more popular than I thought they'd be. I thought they might be a bit niche."

"Doesn't look like it. Bar takings should be sky high tonight for old John there, bless him."

It was the interval, and they took deep breaths to recover. "My God, I haven't laughed so much in years!" said Becki.

"No, not since they kicked out Liz Truss!" added Lizzie. "Shall I go and get us top ups?"

"Yes please, sis." She handed her empty glass over. "I'll nip to the loo. I don't want to risk a full bladder when Big Bertha's doing her stuff again. Not at my age!"

The second half of the show started and Big Bertha came back on stage after an elaborate costume change, In this new skin-tight bright white dress, she had six inch heels on and white feathers on the top of her head that almost touched the lighting rig above her.

"Do you like me new frock?" she asked in a broad Yorkshire accent, bright red lips shining across in the spotlight. "I said - do you like me new frock?" Everyone cheered. "Oh, that's better. I thought you'd all died in the break. So, my new frock, yes. It was going to be a plain little number, but in the interval, I unexpectedly got me end away with an ostrich and this was the result."

Becki and Lizzie laughed until they cried. As the night went on, Big Bertha got ruder and funnier. "Now, I need a volunteer," she said from the stage. The lights shone on the audience and she made a big show of looking around the tables. "Now do I see a willing victim somewhere? Oh no, did I say victim. I meant volunteer. Of course."

Suddenly the spotlight was shining on Becki and Lizzie, who were sitting at their little table handily near the front.

"Ah, you two!" said Bertha coming down off the stage, tottering on her super high heels. "So, are you best friends, sisters or lesbians?"

Lizzie said, "All three of those for me, two for her."

"Ah right, well I'll take the lesbian then. Best chance for me to pull."

She took Lizzie by the hand and helped her up the three steps to the stage. Becki got her phone out and set it to video mode. Dan and the kids could watch it later. She tried to control her laughing so her phone wasn't jumping up and down too much while she was recording.

"Now, what's yer name, chuck?"

"Lizzie."

"Lizzie the lesbian. Fabulous. Now, are you wearing any lipstick?"

"No," Lizzie shook her head. She hadn't bothered putting any on that evening.

"Oh I thought you were wearing that Nearly There shade. Nearly there, but you washed it off with yer first pint, is that it? Well, come here." Bertha gave her an exaggerated kiss on the lips. "There you go. Sharing is caring. You're wearing mine now.

196

Prostitute pink, it's called. One of my favourite lipsticks. It's great for pulling," She looked at the audience. "Pulling teeth in this fucking pub!"

Poor Lizzie was up on the stage for a good ten minutes and Becki had tears running down her cheeks. She was absolutely hilarious and Lizzie didn't seem to mind it too much. Becki was just relieved Bertha hadn't picked her. She'd have hated being the centre of attention. Luckily her younger sister was much happier in that position.

Lizzie came off stage to a big round of applause from the audience and was presented with a huge bouquet of flowers from Big Bertha. "Oh, you were brilliant, sis. Absolutely brilliant!" Becki went to the bar to get two more large gins. She thought Lizzie could definitely do with one.

An hour or so later, not long before closing time, a slim man in his mid-thirties came over to them. "I just wanted to thank you," he said in a soft voice. They looked at him, but they didn't know him. What on earth was he thanking them for? He bent down to their level and said "I'm Bertha. Well, I'm Billy now, but I was Bertha."

"Oh my God, I never recognised you, I'm sorry."

Billy was wearing a crisp pastel pink shirt and smart tight jeans with expensive looking trainers. His hair was short and a pale blond colour. "No, that's the idea. I don't like being recognised as myself. But I just wanted to pop over and check you were okay. I know some people aren't keen to go on stage, but you looked like you'd be fine." He winked at Lizzie.

"I was. Thank you. I enjoyed it. You're amazing."

"Thanks, that's okay then. You both look after yourselves." He kissed both their hands and sashayed through the middle of the room, no-one noticing him except John at the bar, who gave him a grin and a wave. "See you soon!" he shouted as Billy left the pub without a fuss.

"What a sweet man!" said Becki.

"He really was. And what an evening!"

Dan

The three of them were almost at the end of a particularly long and irritating game of Monopoly when they heard the key in the door.

"Fabulous," he said as Lizzie and Becki walked in. "You've saved me."

"Ah, the wonders of Monopoly."

"Yes, it's been one of those games where someone's been close to bankruptcy then another player's landed on their property and saved them. It's been up and down, backwards and forwards for hours. At least we can stop playing now you're back."

"Oh, don't stop on our behalf!" urged Lizzie with a mischievous grin. "I'm sure we all want to know who's going to win." She put the kettle on and put a herbal tea bag in her mug, before asking what everyone else wanted to drink.

Becki let the dog out for a wee, then fed Trudi and Flora. "How have the pets been?"

"Good as gold," replied Dan. "They get on so well together, don't they? They've been snuggled up in the cat bed together a lot of the time."

"Oh, they do that, yes."

"I'd been going to suggest that as you had Trudi, Freddie and I would take Flora home."

A few pairs of unhappy eyes glared at him. He put his hands up in defence. "It's okay though, I realise Trudi and Flora need to be together and it would be cruel to separate them. So, we'll just have to go with Plan B instead."

"And what's that when it's home?" asked Becki, accepting a cup of hot tea gratefully from her sister.

"We'll just have to work towards all getting a place together," explained Dan. "You, me, the kids, the dog and the kitten."

"That sounds like an excellent idea to me, kids, what do you think?"

"Yay!" Freddie and Jemima stood up holding each other's arms and did a kind of cheering, jumping, turning dance.

"I think they're happy!" commented Lizzie.

"That makes all of us then!" said Becki, going over to kiss Dan.

"Oh," said Becki. "That kiss reminded me. Aunt Lizzie got a kiss tonight."

"Oh yes?"

"Don't worry, she wasn't being unfaithful to Ebele."

"No I certainly wasn't." The sisters laughed together, remembering the hilarity of their evening,

"Come on, let us into the big secret," pleaded Dan.

Becki got her phone out and played them the video. After all the laughter had died down – which admittedly took a while – and they had all admired Lizzie's flowers which she'd placed in a glass vase she'd found in a cupboard, Jemima suddenly stopped laughing. "Mum. How did you show us that video without Wi-Fi?"

"Ah. Yes. About that. When I was talking to John, the landlord of the pub, he told me that Silver Sands Bay has some kind of shared Wi-Fi between all the arcades, chip shop, pub, caravan sites and whatever. The code is apparently written up in all those places."

"Well, I've never seen it."

"No, but then maybe we haven't been looking."

"Did he tell you what it was, Mum?"

"He did, I wrote it down."

The kids grabbed at the piece of paper, both putting the code into their mobiles at super-fast speed. Suddenly all their phones were beeping and pinging, jumping into life again, assaulting the senses.

"Do you know," commented Dan. "I think there are definite advantages to not knowing the Wi-Fi code."

"I agree," said Becki. "I've rather enjoyed being without the internet."

"Did John tell you about that tonight then?" questioned Lizzie.

"No, it was at the quiz night. I'd told him I thought one of the answers wasn't correct and he said I should check it on my phone, because sometimes they do get things wrong. When I said I couldn't check it because we had no Wi-Fi, he wrote down the code for me. I only just remembered!"

"Mum! That was days ago! You could have told us sooner." whined Jemima.

"Oh, come on, Jem, you've got to admit we've had a lovely holiday, with or without the sodding internet."

And they all agreed they had.

Then went back to scrolling through Facebook, Twitter and Instagram.

CHAPTER NINE

Becki

It was Tuesday - the day Lizzie went home. She had packed up her things the previous evening and had filled her little car up with them an hour ago. The caravan was already looking emptier. They'd been so lucky to have had these weeks together, but Becki was upset her little sister was leaving. She knew there was absolutely no point in asking her to stay, because Ebele was back in London the next day and she knew they had been separated too long already. Besides, they had wedding plans to organise.

Lizzie came in from outside, Jemima and Trudi just behind. "I'll have a tea before I go," Lizzie said, clicking the kettle on and rinsing the mugs they'd used earlier. Becki noticed Jemima's eyes were red and realised she'd been crying. They'd all miss her, the animals too.

They sat on the sofas for the final time. "I'm going to miss this place," said Lizzie in a strained voice. "It's been so good being here with you all, meeting Dan and Freddie. So lovely."

When Dan and Freddie themselves arrived to say their farewells, they found the three of them hugging each other in a kind of amorphous, soggy mass of tears. "Oh no, we can't have this," Dan stepped up to them. "Come on, girls. It won't be long before you'll see each other again. We've got the wedding to look forward to, for starters."

The three females all turned to look at him at the same time. "Now Dan," mock-warned Lizzie. "You're not planning to upstage me and Ebele by you two getting married first, are you?"

"No, no, no, don't worry about that. We've got to find a place to buy and all sorts first before we can even think about getting married." He paused theatrically. "We'll be at least a couple of weeks behind you!"

Becki nudged him in the ribs. "Hey! You haven't even proposed yet."

"And when I do, remind me not to get down on one knee. You know how difficult it was last time I was kneeling in front of you." Lizzie raised her eyebrows comically. "No, Lizzie that's not what I meant." He grinned cheekily at her.

"Hey, I might get to be a bridesmaid twice!"

"Yes, Jemima. We could even use the same dress, save a bit of money."

"Cheapskate!"

"Oh, are we both going for the same neon pink theme then?" Lizzie winked at her older sister.

"Absolutely! I've heard it's all on trend nowadays. The retro look is back!"

The banter continued until Lizzie checked the time. "I'm so sorry, guys, but I'm going to have to go. It's a fair distance and I'm bound to need to stop for food and toilet breaks a couple of times on the way back, so I'd better get myself off."

They all had hugs and kisses, including the two pets. Dan stayed in the caravan with Trudi and Flora while Becki, Jemima and Freddie went to wave Lizzie off as she drove out of the caravan park in her little pink Mini and off in the direction of home.

"Oh, it's nice to think she'll be with Ebele again tomorrow," said Jemima. Becki realised her daughter was trying to keep positive and joined in with the theme.

"Yes, our loss is her gain. I'm so pleased they worked things out. It would have been such a shame if they'd split up over a simple mistake, Lizzie thinking Ebele was finishing with her when in fact, that was the last thing on her mind."

Dan coughed pointedly behind them. "Yes, funny how things like that happen, isn't it?" He drew Becki in for a long, lingering kiss as Jemima and Freddie busied themselves in the lounge, fussing over the dog and kitten.

Becki

Their last couple of days at Silver Sands Bay seemed to whizz past. They all had a final chip shop tea, both Becki and Jemima giving Jean a big cuddle and swapping contact details. When Jean saw their address, she said "Oh, I've got a brother who lives in Knaresborough. I don't get chance to see him often because this place is a full-time job, but we do shut for a month in winter so I might well be up near you."

"Well, if you are, please give us a ring. I'd love to meet up with you again."

"I'm sure you will, love, I'm sure you will."

The Wednesday was a glorious day, temperatures in the high twenties but with a pleasant breeze on the beach. They sat there with books and phones and a copy of the local newspaper, happily relaxing in each other's company.

"I hope Flora will be okay," said Becki. "It's the first time we've left her alone. I hope she doesn't scratch anywhere."

"Oh, yes, about that," replied Jemima shyly. She reached into her pastel pink satchel and brought out a sleeping bundle of black fur with a bright white tummy. "I didn't think she was quite ready to be left alone yet. She seems to like my bag too, must be the swinging motion of me walking, it rocked her to sleep."

"Thank God it wasn't the goldfish I won at the fair in 1978. That wouldn't have survived in your bag like that!"

"No, Dad, especially if the cat had been in there at the same time!"

What a happy family they looked. No one walking past would know they were two families – a single dad with his son and a single mum with her daughter. But they weren't single anymore. Soon they would be one big hopefully happy family. A modern, blended family, but a family, nonetheless.

Dan

The packing was all done and everything was in the car. Dan hated farewells. It had been difficult enough saying goodbye to Lizzie, but this was going to be even worse – even though they'd arranged to meet up the following week. Apart from the aberration caused by Melanie's crisis, they hadn't been apart much at all over the six weeks of the summer holiday.

He locked up the caravan and pocketed the keys, ready to hand them into the man at the Reception shed on their way out. He went over to Becki's caravan where everyone else was. He could hear the laughter from a couple of caravans away and paused momentarily to listen to it. He could distinguish each of their laughs – his Freddie's, high at the moment, but it would soon get deeper. Jemima's laugh was still the giggle of a young girl, her mum's definitely a tone deeper and, he thought to himself, rather a sexy laugh too. He liked Becki's laugh. Well, he liked everything about Becki, to be fair.

He sighed, realising he could prolong things no longer. They had to go soon, there were things to get ready at home in Wetherby. He was back at work on Monday and Freddie was due to start his new secondary school. There was school uniform to iron and his work clothes to get ready, packed lunches to make, school books and P.E. kit to get organised. Back to normal. Well, almost. This new normal was a much more pleasant prospect that it had been six weeks ago. He wasn't on his own anymore. He was part of a new relationship, a new family.

As he walked up the steps into the caravan, he heard arguing coming from the kids in the lounge.

"I'm getting the biggest bedroom," Freddie was saying.

"What, Freddie? How does that work out?"

"When we all live together. I'm getting the biggest bedroom."

"You're so not! I'm getting the biggest bedroom!"

"Why do you deserve it, not me? I'm the oldest!"

"Only by two months and anyway, I've got loads of clothes and make up and, er, girlie hair things to put somewhere. I need loads of storage space!"

Dan and Becki came into the lounge just as the kids started having a pillow fight with the sofa cushions. Trudi and Flora had retreated safely to the cat bed, well out of the way.

"Look at those two," said Dan quietly. "Already fighting like brother and sister."

Becki smiled up at him and squeezed his hand.

EPILOGUE

Eleven Months Later

It was July again, the start of yet another long summer holiday. Becki, Jemima and Trudi walked down Tall Trees Caravan Park looking out for a familiar caravan. Trudi started pulling the lead one way, as she recognised where they had stayed the previous year. "No, not that one!" Becki pulled her back. "Over here!"

As they headed over towards the brown and white painted caravan, Dan appeared with the keys. "Here we go, the old boy was just finishing the end of a race, so I had to wait. He was happy though, won forty quid on it."

Unlocking the door, they all walked up the two steps and put their things down. "I'll go back and get the rest of the luggage," Dan said.

"In a minute, love. There's no hurry." Becki gave him a long kiss. "Isn't it lovely to be back here? A whole year…"

"And what a year it's been, Mrs. Armstrong."

Freddie put the car carrier down on the sofa. Flora was miaowing loudly. "I think she's had enough of being shut up in that thing. Shall we close the door and let her out?"

"Yes, that's a good idea. Poor thing, it's a long journey for a little cat."

Jemima shut the door, carrying her big bag of art stuff inside. "I'll put this under the bed for now. I'm having the single, aren't I? Freddie, you're kipping on the sofa cushions in the lounge."

"Oh, that's not fair! I thought it was the other way round."

He opened the door of the cat carrier and Flora came out, looked around her, stretched then did a wee all over the sofa. "Oh, not again, kitten cat!" moaned Dan, going to the kitchen to get the cleaning stuff out.

"I'm starving!"

"You're always starving, Jem. Shall we go to the chippy?"

"Yeah, that's a good idea. Freddie can stay here with the animals, I'll get the rest of the bags from the car then we can all sit down to eat," said Dan. "Come to think of it, I'm starving too. Tell Jean we'll have our usuals, please!"

"Will do."

Becki and Jemima headed out of the caravan site, noting the shower and toilet block had been repainted and modernised since the previous year. "Ooh look at that, Mum, that's posh!"

"He must have had a few wins on the horses!"

As they got to the street they remembered so well, it started to rain. "Bloody typical!" Jemima moaned, as her mum looked heavenwards and shook her head.

"It'll only be a summer shower. It'll have probably stopped by the time we get back."

Luckily there wasn't a queue outside The Inn Plaice for once, so they walked straight in. "Hey!" greeted Jean, reaching across the counter to give them a big cuddle each. "How are you guys?"

"All good, thanks." Becki wiggled her shiny gold wedding ring over the counter.

"Oh, look at that, it's gorgeous! I'm sorry I couldn't get to your wedding, but it was packed here and I just couldn't take the time off. But I saw your photos on Facebook, you looked beautiful. And Jemima, your bridesmaid's dress was stunning!"

"Aww thanks Jean, it was a lovely day."

"Are your sister and her wife doing okay?"

"Yes, they're really happy, thanks. And – more good news – Ebele is expecting their baby!"

"Well," Jean said. "While we're on the subject of good news, I wondered if you'd be available in early August."

"We'll be here then. Why?"

"Well, it turns out you aren't the only ones falling in love in Silver Sands Bay."

"Oh."

Suddenly the door behind the counter opened and John the pub landlord came in, hairnet over his grey hair. "Oh, hello loves, great to see you again. You back for the summer?"

Becki nodded. "So…?"

"Yes, girls. Meet my fiancé, John. Well, you know him of course, but yes, we got together last September, not long after you'd all gone home. It turns out that little chat I had with you on the beach, Becki, reminded me of what I was really feeling for someone. And it turned out he felt the same too."

"Ah that's just perfect, I'm so happy for you both."

A few more people had joined the queue and Jean realised she'd been chatting for too long. "Right, we'll have a big catch up another time. What do you want to eat?"

"Three lots of fish, chips and peas please. Jemima, what do you want?"

"I've got some halloumi in for you, Jem, I was hoping you'd be coming back."

"Ah, sorry Jean. No halloumi for me. I'm vegan now."

"Since when?" asked her mum.

"Last Wednesday."

"You never told me!"

"You never asked!"

And the rain stopped falling, the sun came out and the sand on the beach shone silver.

THE END

ACKNOWLEDGEMENTS

My first and biggest thank you must go to Jessica Redland. It was studying her course – the RNA's Writing a Novel or Series in a Coastal or Country Setting – that inspired me to write this story. Not only is she one of my favourite authors, but she's such a lovely person and a truly inspirational tutor.

I'd also like to thank some of the teachers I had in the 1980s, who encouraged me to write and nurtured any talent I showed -

Mr Gowenlock and Mr Fear at St Faith and St Martin's Middle School, Lincoln.

Mrs Wilks and Mr C Smith at William Farr C of E Comprehensive School, Welton, Lincs.

Mr Ross and Mr Bridgewater at De Aston School, Market Rasen, Lincs.

I'd also like to thank Paul O'Grady. He died while I was writing this book and I never realised how much I loved him until afterwards. He has inspired me in a few parts of this book. ITV showed an episode of *Paul O'Grady – For The Love of Dogs* to commemorate his sad death and in the programme, there was a rescue dog called Flora. So the story of the rescue kitten called Flora in *Starting Again in Silver Sands Bay* was inspired by that. I'm sure Paul would have approved.

I had already mentioned the drag artist before Paul died, but when Big Bertha appeared, I'm sure I was channelling my inner Lily Savage somewhere. Sadly I never got to meet Paul, but I was in a pub in Portsmouth in the mid-1990s when my friend pointed out a quiet, slim man sitting on his own. He said "You see that man over there. That's Lily Savage." We didn't approach him, because he was alone and seemed rather reserved, but my inspiration for Billy came from that memory.

Rest in peace Paul O'Grady (1955-2023). I hope you know how much we loved you.

Another huge thank you goes to Patrick White who designed the beautiful book cover. He was endlessly patient as I kept wanting it changed, the kids looking older or younger, the colours or the font altered. It took a while to get it perfect, but he never complained. I owe him a pint. Or three.

Thanks to Bob Acrey for reading early versions of the book.

I need to thank my dad Peter Brown, for always being there to talk to about writing.

Finally I'd like to thank my author friends who make this writing journey so much fun, it does make a big difference knowing you've got a team rooting for you. I know I'll forget someone so I apologise in advance, but a big shout out to Anita Faulkner, the Chick Lit and Prosecco Facebook group, Abigail Yardimci, Helga Jensen, Heidi Swain herself and the Heidi Swain and Friends Facebook group and to my new writing friends at Starfish Writers 2023.

Much love!

Karen xxx

Karen Louise Hollis was born in Lincoln in 1969. She lives with her mother, son and a black and white cat called Socks. When she's not writing, she's probably reading, sewing or catching up with the latest thriller on Catch-up TV.

If you enjoyed this book, remember to check out Karen Louise's first novel *Welcome to Whitlock Close* and her other books over on Amazon and at karenlouisehollis.co.uk

Find her on social media at –

TWITTER : @KarenLNHollis

INSTAGRAM: @karenlouisehollis

BLOG: iheartbooks.blog

If you've enjoyed this book, please leave a positive review on Amazon, Goodreads and other sites you use.

Printed in Great Britain
by Amazon

21367658R00123